# CHAOTIC CORGIS

A COZY CORGI MYSTERY

MILDRED ABBOTT

WINGS OF INK PUBLICATIONS, LLC

CHAOTIC CORGIS

Mildred Abbott

*for*

*Alastair Tyler*

Cover, Logo, Chapter Heading Designer: A.J. Corza - SeeingStatic.com

Main Editor: Desi Chapman

2nd Editor: Ann Attwood

3rd Editor: Corrine Harris

Recipe and photo provided by: Biscotti Hound - BiscottiHound.com

Visit Mildred's Webpage: MildredAbbott.com

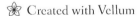 Created with Vellum

ABOUT CHAOTIC CORGIS

At the height of the summer season, Estes Park explodes with people, wildlife, fireworks, and... murder.

The Cozy Corgi Bookshop and Bakery is buzzing with tourists, and Winifred Page and her quirky corgi, Watson, celebrate the Fourth of July picnicking with family and friends—of the human and four-legged variety. As summer blooms with romance for Fred and Sergeant Branson Wexler, murder lurks around the corner.

With a friend's life in danger, Fred and Watson doggedly pursue the investigation, even as Fred finds herself once again at odds with the police department. But caring for two chaotic corgis while navigating emotions from the past in the midst of solving a mystery might be too much, and Fred hits a roadblock.

As relationships are tested and secrets exposed, Fred might lose more than one person she loves...

An earthquake rumbled the bed, shaking me awake. I stared at the ceiling, which was neither rumbling nor shaking.

Not an earthquake. Obviously. Colorado wasn't prone to earthquakes. Of course, neither was Missouri where I'd moved from eight months before, so who knew why I thought I was in the middle of an earthquake.

The bed shook again, but there was no rattle of dishes nor trembling of walls.

I glanced over to find two red, pointy fox ears poking over the edge of the mattress, accompanied by a wet, black nose.

Okay, kind of an earthquake.

Watson chuffed, pounded his front paws on the edge of the mattress, and snorted.

I rolled toward him. "You're making some very ungentlemanly noises this morning."

He snorted again.

As I reached out to pat his head, I glanced at the clock, then glared at Watson. "Seriously? *Five* in the morning?"

He cocked his head as if determining whether I had a valid point. Apparently, I didn't, as he chuffed again and smacked his front paws on the bed once more.

I couldn't help but laugh and gave in to petting him. "You know, if you were an inch taller you wouldn't get away with such shenanigans, but waking up to nothing but pointy ears and an adorable dog nose isn't a half bad way to be disturbed. Better than an earthquake at any rate."

Watson gave a quick lick on the tip of my nose, pushed off the side of the bed, plopped down on his little corgi legs to the wood bedroom floor, and then trotted over to the doorway to look back demandingly over his shoulder.

"You know, I need to teach you how to make breakfast." I looked at the clock again, considering. I could ignore him, shove pillows on either side of my head and drown out the world until the alarm went off. But... he *had* given me puppy kisses on the nose, a very un-Watson thing to do. I supposed I should reward such affection, even if it was complete manipulation. Plus... the quicker I got out of bed, the quicker I got coffee.

Within a few minutes, the nectar of the gods was brewing, filling the small kitchen of my log cabin with a cozy aroma. I fried eggs over the mint-green oven that came straight from the sixties, while the faintest crack of dawn filtered through the lemon-yellow and lime-green tie-dyed curtains with a pink flamingo pattern over them that came straight from my mother and hippie-dippy stepfather. Watson sat at my feet, staring expectantly. If a person had to wake up before the sun, this was the perfect place to do it.

Finishing up cooking, I prepared plates for Watson and myself, then glanced at the clock again, before smiling at Watson. "We're having breakfast on the porch this morning."

Watson trotted along behind, chuffing irritably every so often as I gathered up a blanket and book, before settling onto the driftwood bench and lowering Watson's plate to the floor. Though it was July, the morning was cool and crisp. Surrounded by a forest of pines and aspens, with the Rocky Mountain peaks towering overhead, I snuggled into the blanket, and propped the book on my lap as I ate.

No, not a bad way to wake up at all.

"Revenge is a dish best served cold. I warned you weeks ago." I glanced both ways on Elkhorn Avenue, and since the light at the intersection was red, I jaywalked with Watson through the bumper-to-bumper summer traffic. Once safely on the other side, I addressed my corgi again. "Well, mister, it's cold and it's time."

One of the many tourists crowding the streets of downtown Estes Park offered a wide-eyed stare from over their triple-scoop ice cream cone and then gave me a wide berth. Another, apparently not thrown off by me having a conversation with my dog, bent down with a flourish to pet Watson.

Watson flinched, huffed, and backpedaled to take shelter beneath my brown-and-pea-green broomstick skirt.

The man straightened, looking offended.

I attempted an apologetic shrug. "Sorry about that. Watson's a little particular who he lets pet him."

The man's expression soured further, and then

he, too, gave us a sizable distance and disappeared into the hordes.

I suppose that sounded insulting, though it was true enough. Watson was finicky at the best of times, but the endless number of people at high-tide tourist season made him even grumpier than usual.

Watson poked his head out from under my skirt, saw the coast was clear, and emerged once more, leaving a cloud of dog hair rising between us. Cutting his way through the tourists' feet, he attempted to lead me to Cabin and Hearth, the local upscale log cabin furniture store.

"Oh no. No fancy dog bones for you." I pointed to the shop next door when Watson glared back at me. "Revenge, remember? It's time for you to pay up."

Proving his senses were spread thin, Watson followed me easily for a few steps until we almost reached the door to the pet shop before he balked and demonstrated just how powerful his tiny legs were by pulling me back in the direction of the cabin store.

"Watson!" I'd been unprepared for his sudden jolt and was actually maneuvered a few steps away before I managed to get a better grip on his leash.

His pointy ears drooped partially. Not to the

level of a full-blown apology, but enough to play up the cute factor.

"Nope. Not gonna work. You've had this coming." I snapped my fingers and pointed for him to come to my feet.

He considered.

Watson was my pet. I was his master. That was how the pet ownership gig went.

However, in true stubborn corgi nature, Watson wasn't overly convinced of that fact.

Honestly, neither was I.

To my surprise, with a huff, he lifted his nose in the air, saving face, and trotted over to sit at my feet.

"Good boy." I attempted to not let my astonishment show—better for him to think there wasn't another option, even if we both knew better. "If you fight against this, it'll just take longer."

Another tourist bumped into me, muttered an apology, and kept going.

Since moving to Estes Park, I'd been looking forward to tourist season getting into high gear. But now, though I was enjoying the mild summer weather in the Colorado mountain town, I realized I shared a bit more of Watson's grumpy old man personality than I cared to admit. I turned back toward the front door of Paws, but a movement from the pet shop's window caught my attention, and I leaned a little closer to see inside.

Through a slight glare, I saw a couple embracing in the middle of the store. They were indiscernible. The woman had her arms thrown around the man's neck as she stood on tiptoe, her long fall of blonde hair swinging at the movement.

Maybe Watson would get his reprieve after all. I didn't want to walk into the middle of that.

Just as I was about to pull away, the man lifted his face, and his eyes met mine.

I gave a little jolt. It was Paulie Mertz, the pet shop owner.

Not seeming the slightest bit thrown off by being caught in the hug, he beamed, lifted one hand from the woman's back, and motioned for me to come in.

I hesitated, then gave a nod before looking down at Watson. "You have some kind of magical powers, don't you? You're already paying me back for doing this."

Clearly over me, Watson didn't bother to acknowledge my words, but he followed toward the door without any more struggling.

I took a steadying breath before going inside. Over the past month or so, I'd made a more active attempt at being Paulie's friend. He'd even hung out with Katie, Leo, and me on a few different occasions. Though there were times he was off-putting and awkward, I truly had begun to care about him. However, he'd retained that platonic, nearly eunuch-like position in my mind. The thought of being in the same room with him and a lady friend was akin to walking in on your grandparents in a compromising situation. Just, eww, and... no.

When Watson and I stepped inside, all such thoughts vanished at the instant cacophony of barking and howling. The commotion set off the screech of birds from somewhere in the back. Paulie's two corgis, Flotsam and Jetsam, tore from the other side of the shop, stumbling over each other in their haste to get to Watson.

Once more, Watson took shelter beneath my skirt, and not for the first time, my body doubled as a corgi playground—or corgi cage-fight arena, depending on which one of the participants you asked.

Bending down, I took hold of the red one's collar —Jetsam, if I recalled correctly. Even as I pulled him away from Watson, he wriggled and squirmed while simultaneously bathing my forearm in slimy kisses.

Not worth it. Most definitely not worth it. This was more of a revenge on myself than Watson.

"Fred! Watson!" Paulie hurried over from the woman and wrapped his thin arms around me in a friendly embrace. "So nice to see you. What a pleasant surprise."

I attempted to return the hug while snagging the tricolor's collar but only managed to set Jetsam free once more to barrel back beneath my skirt. "Paulie." I blew out a breath. "A little help, please?"

"Oh, of course." He released me, clapped his hands, and cried out cheerfully as if there was no skirmish at all beneath us. "Boys! Snacks!" Then he hurried over to the counter.

The corgi shenanigans didn't falter until they heard the crinkling of a plastic bag being opened, and then Flotsam and Jetsam tore out from underneath my feet so quickly one of them nearly took my skirt in his haste to get to his master.

There was a giggle from across the room, and I looked over to see the curvy blonde grinning at us. "So cute."

I'd forgotten about her. Forgot about everything as one does when about to become a double amputee. "Yes, adorable." I lifted my skirt slightly and peered beneath.

Watson glared, making it clear I was going to be paying for this for days.

Most definitely not worth it.

Flotsam and Jetsam had wandered off with their treats, and typically they didn't bother Watson again after that. The duration of the chaos seemed to lessen with every interaction between the three dogs, though not the intensity. I kept waiting for the two of them to remember that my little man was nothing more than a grump and was never going to play with them the way they wanted, but they were tenacious. Although, I supposed it had worked well for their father, who'd been equally, if not more subtly, determined to strike up a friendship.

Paulie came over once more and held a dog bone toward my feet. "Sorry about that, Watson. They just love you, that's all."

Watson deigned to sniff at the dog treat but then proved just how offended he was by retreating once more.

"Well, you can have this whenever you want it." Paulie bent a little farther, and with his true lack of social awareness, shoved the dog bone beneath the hem of my skirt before standing once more. "They really do love him."

"I know they do." I attempted a smile. "Sorry for the disruption. I wasn't trying to... intrude on anything." I flicked my gaze toward the woman.

Though Paulie looked confused, the blonde hurried over and extended a small hand in my direction. "Oh, not at all. Don't ever be sorry for such a cuteness overload. I'm Melody."

I shook her hand, but before I could offer my name, loud crunching sounded from beneath my skirt. It seemed Watson was getting over his offense.

"Cuter and cuter." The woman giggled as she pulled her hand away and then gave Paulie a quick squeeze. "And you're not interrupting. Paulie was just making my dreams come true."

Unable to stop myself, I glanced at her ring finger. Sure enough, a large diamond glistened. I hadn't even realized Paulie had been dating anyone.

"Don't you mean Ethel, Beatrice, Cinnamon, Angel, Leroy, Finnegan, and Sherbet's dreams come true?" Paulie winked at the blonde.

"They're one and the same. Their dreams are my dreams. Just like you are with your boys." She gave him another squeeze before grinning at me. "And like you are with your cute little one, I'm sure."

I started to nod in agreement, then paused. "You know, I think I'm missing something."

"Come here, I'll show you." Paulie took my hand and led me to the far side of the store.

As his shelter moved away, Watson picked up what was left of his snack and retreated to a corner.

"Melody just purchased the Cat Castle Deluxe." Paulie practically vibrated with excitement as he gestured toward the structure that took up a good fifteen feet of the wall space. I'd seen cat trees before, but this was like a hundred of them put together. Cylinders, ladders, towers, ropes, and wheels were all jumbled together to form the shape of a castle. I had to admit, it looked like fun, if you were a cat. There were a couple of hammocks dangling between different turrets and little nooks and crannies that led to secret passages among the sections. To top it off, a large dragon by the drawbridge appeared to be made out of the material cats liked to scratch.

Suddenly Watson's moody disposition and treat obsession seemed relatively easygoing. "Wow. That is... something."

"Isn't it? The kids are just going to love it." Melody stared at the contraption with the gaze of a lover. "I've been wanting it since Paulie got it in a couple of months ago but couldn't justify the expense. But our anniversary is coming up, so I figure my husband and I can afford the splurge."

It finally all clicked into place.

She and Paulie weren't having some secret affair

that had just ended with an engagement. He'd simply made a big sale. Wow, and to think I prided myself on my deductive skills.

"So...." I thought back. "Ethel and... Leroy must be your cats?"

"Yes." She nodded and began counting them off on her fingers. "Angel, Beatrice, Cinnamon, Ethel, Finnegan, Leroy, and Sherbet are our babies."

I gaped at her. "*Seven*? You have seven cats?"

Melody nodded again, her pride obvious. "Yes. All Persians. And all with prestigious pedigrees."

Persians! Seven of them! "Wow. And here I thought my life was ruled by pet hair."

She chuckled. "You just have to stay on top of it." Her bright blue eyes flicked toward my cream-colored peasant blouse, doubtlessly finding multiple examples of how I was very far from staying on top of it. "It helps if you carry around a lint roller."

"Yes. I suppose it would. I have one in the glove compartment of my car, but honestly, I've given up. If you can't love me with dog hair, then you can't love me at all."

"I agree with you on that one." Paulie gave the cat castle an affectionate pat before turning back to me. "It's unusual for you to bring Watson in lately.

Did you come for something specific or just to say hi?"

I'd nearly forgotten. "Oh, right." I glanced over at the corner where Watson had finished his snack and was now snoring in the afternoon sunlight. Based on only hearing the soft chirping of birds, squeaking of rodent wheels, and gurgling of aquariums in the background of the store, I assumed Flotsam and Jetsam were napping as well. Maybe Watson would let go of his grudge earlier than I feared. "I wanted to get a Fourth of July outfit for Watson. I thought the tourists might enjoy my little mascot looking like Uncle Sam or something."

Before Paulie could respond, Melody sucked in her breath. "Oh. That's how I know you. You're Fred, right? The lady who owns the Cozy Corgi Bookshop. You have the best bakery in town."

"Yes, I am, and thank you." I smiled at her, pleased. "Although the bakery part is owned by my best friend, Katie. I can't take any credit for that, but I have to agree; I think she's the best baker I've ever met."

The pretty blonde patted her flat stomach. "My husband and I came in a couple of times when we moved to town in January, but now it's a rare occasion. We try to be healthy."

I was surprised I didn't remember seeing her in the shop. Though, since opening the bookstore, there'd been many times I'd been pulled away with events a little more pressing than books and pastries. "Be that as it may, Katie and I both appreciate your business when you and your husband decide to indulge."

Her blue eyes brightened. "That's not a bad idea. If we're splurging on the cats for our anniversary, I suppose we should splurge for ourselves as well. Maybe we'll come in and pick up a cake or something from Katie. A small one."

"I'm sure she'd love that." I returned my attention to Paulie. "Watson and I can wait if you want to finish up with Melody. There's no rush."

"Oh no, you go ahead." Melody jumped in before Paulie could respond. "Once I come in here, I stay forever. There are just so many fun and adorable little cat toys to choose from. Jared and I, he's my husband, try to be sensible and not go overboard, so it always takes me a while to choose which one I want to get." She gave the cat castle a pat of her own. "This is a surprise, and I won't pick it up for a few more days, so they need a little something to tide them over in the meantime."

I wasn't sure how the cat castle could ever be

qualified as sensible, but I was glad for Paulie that he seemed to be making what was surely a substantial sale. "All right, then. If you're sure. Thank you."

"I insist. And your little one is going to look absolutely adorable as Uncle Sam." She waggled her fingers toward a sleeping Watson and then got lost to the selection of toys.

Paulie slid his arm through mine as we walked over to the dog section. "You must have a death wish. I thought you said Watson would murder you in your sleep if you ever tried to put an outfit on him."

"It's payback. And I told him it was coming. Remember my birthday cake?"

He chuckled. "Oh yes. I suppose he does have some payback coming."

Katie had thrown a birthday bash at the bookstore when I turned thirty-nine at the end of May. Just as she'd been about to cut the cake, Watson displayed one of his rare feats of athletic ability, bounded onto a nearby chair, then the countertop, and helped himself to the first bite.

"In his defense, you said yourself you hadn't given him any snacks all day. He was desperate."

I leveled my gaze on Paulie. "It wasn't like I starved him. He had breakfast and lunch. I just hadn't given any snacks. I knew he'd get a boatload during the party, if nothing else from all the crumbs people would drop on the floor. There has to be a line somewhere, or he'll be the size of Flotsam and Jetsam rolled into one." As we stopped in front of the section of dog outfits, I began to second-guess myself. Revenge or not, trying to stuff Watson into a full-body hotdog suit really was inviting my own murder. Chickening out, I reached for a tiny red, white, and blue top hat that had strings to secure under a dog's jaw. "How about this instead? A compromise of sorts."

"Yeah. That's a good idea." He plucked the hat from my hands and checked the label. "However, this is more for a dog the size of a Chihuahua or a toy poodle." Paulie bent forward and shuffled through the other outfits. "I don't have the right one for a corgi, but I can order one. It could be here by the third; would that work?"

I probably shouldn't mess with it. Even with the hat tied on his head, it was highly doubtful Watson would leave it alone for more than five minutes, but it really would be cute. Maybe I could get him to leave it on long enough for a photograph in any case. "Yes, that would be great. Thank you."

Paulie sucked in a breath. "I have a great idea!

Are you guys still coming to my softball game that afternoon?"

"We are. Katie and I are leaving the twins in charge of the bookshop and bakery." We'd debated about the intelligence of leaving our new employees for the first time unassisted on what was destined to be one of the busiest days of the year, but it had seemed so important to Paulie that we attend, we couldn't turn him down.

"Awesome! I wasn't going to join again this year, but since Declan's not a part of it any longer—" Paulie's eyes widened. "Crap. Probably shouldn't say things like that."

I patted his arm. "You're okay, Paulie. Declan was horrible to you and several others. I'm glad you're trying it again. Between that and bird club, your social calendar is getting pretty full lately."

"Yeah, it is." His smile was so bright that even with his yellowish teeth, it was a thing of beauty. He sighed contentedly. "Anyway, I know you need to get back to the bookshop. I'll order a Statue of Liberty hat for Flotsam and a Betsy Ross hat for Jetsam. It'll be perfect."

The slice of prime rib was the largest I'd ever seen. If the dining room of Pinecone Manor wasn't dripping with upscale mountain-chic class and romantic ambience, from the portion size, I would've assumed it was one of those restaurants that if you eat an entire cow within the hour you got your meal for free and had your picture hung on the wall. The same was true of the baked potato.

"I've wanted to eat here for ages. Thanks for giving me an excuse." Branson Wexler tipped his glass of red wine my direction and took a sip, his bright green eyes sparkling as his gaze stayed on me.

"It's delicious. And you don't have to choose between quality or quantity." I refocused on my dinner. The center of the meat was a little rare for my liking, though I knew that was how prime rib was supposed to be served. I cut around it and pushed the portion to the side before moving on to a more well-done piece.

"Is it too gamy for you? The flavor of elk can be an acquired taste."

Right. Elk. So, in this case, it would have been one of those restaurants where you ate an entire *elk* and you got your meal for free. "No, I got used to all the different types of meats when I'd come up to Estes to visit my grandparents and uncles as a kid. I'm just going to save that little bit for Watson."

Branson practically sputtered and chuckled. "You are something, Winifred Page. I've had dates refuse to eat their meal saying they'd rather have a salad because they were watching their weight, but I've never had a woman save the best part of her dinner for her dog."

I gave an exaggerated shudder. "Salad? You know me better than that. Even if I did have that disposition, Katie baking all day above me would've ruined that ages ago. Why settle for salad when you can have fresh pastry goodness and prime rib?" I poked at the bloody center cut. "But I also want to keep the peace. Watson's still irritable about me dragging him to the pet shop yesterday, and my leaving him home tonight will only add to that. An offering

has to be made if there's going to be any recon-
ciliation."

"I should've picked a restaurant that was dog
friendly, but I wanted tonight to be special." He
slipped his hand inside the inner pocket of his suit
jacket, pulled out a little box, and placed it on the
table between us. "I was planning on giving this to
you for your birthday, but it wasn't ready in time, and
then...." He shrugged. "Well... the timing hasn't felt
right since."

For one terrifying, heart-stopping moment, I
stared at the tiny box, my blood running cold.

There was a ring inside. He was proposing. Holy
Lord, he was proposing!

"Fred." Branson reached across the table and
placed his hand over mine.

I continued to stare at the velvet trap... er... gift.

"Fred." He squeezed my hand as he repeated my
name and smiled gently when I looked up at him.
"It's not a ring."

I glanced back down at the box and then at
Branson once more. It wasn't a ring? Not a proposal?
Of course it wasn't. "Am I that obvious?"

"With as white as you went, you were either
thinking I was getting ready to ask you to marry me
or I'd hidden a bomb in there." He chuckled again.

"And with the tenacity and speed that you've been solving murders, I don't think a bomb would scare you that badly."

I swallowed, trying to get my nerves to resemble that of a normal human being instead of Paulie's hyperactive corgis. "I'm sorry. I hope it's not insulting. It's just that—"

"Fred." Branson squeezed my hand again. "I think you're having the appropriate response if I was really going to propose right now. That would be a little out of the blue, don't you think?"

It most definitely would've been. Not to mention insane, ludicrous, and absolutely terrifying. But with the initial relief of knowing that I wasn't about to endure a marriage proposal, a sliver of irritation entered, though I tried not to let it sound in my voice. "In my defense, you brought me to the most romantic restaurant in Estes Park, the one they literally advertise as the place to propose to your girlfriend, and told me to get all dressed up"—I motioned down at my body, though most of it was hidden by the table —"which required me to go shopping at Silk and Satin to get a new dress."

"You look stunning, by the way." His thumb moved over the back of my hand and his voice dipped to a heated purr.

"Thank you. That's not the point." I waved him off even as I was flattered at the compliment. Katie had taken me dress shopping, demanding I go outside my comfort zone and get something more formfitting and in another shade than my typical earth tones. Considering the amount of pastries Watson and I had been consuming over the past few months, I had to admit, though I was rather surprised, it was a good look on me. *Not* that I was about to trade my broomstick skirts and cowboy boots for designer labels and high heels, but still. "You tell me it's a special occasion and then you put a ring-sized box on the table. What was I supposed to think?"

"Well...." His handsome smile curved to something slightly wicked. "I am hoping this is a special night. We've been dating for a while...."

My pulse rose nearly as much at it had at the sight of the dreaded ring box. It seemed Katie had been right. Pinecone Manor was not only the most romantic restaurant in Estes Park with the best views, but also a bed-and-breakfast. Even though I told her she was crazy, part of me had known, even if I didn't want to think about it. I supposed Branson's expectation or hope wasn't unfounded. We had been dating... going on dates rather... regularly for several months. Most other couples would have crossed that bridge a long time ago. But I'd made it very clear I wanted to go slow. "Branson—"

"Sergeant Wexler, I was so happy when I saw your name on the reservation list for this evening."

Both of us turned to see Meisel Pepper beside our table. She and her husband, Clyde, owned Pinecone Manor. She was tiny enough that even though we were seated, she was directly at eye level.

The older woman flashed me a quick smile. "And it's lovely to have you here too, Ms. Page. Your bookstore is charming." Without waiting for a response, she turned back to Branson. "I just want to thank you for all you do for the town. On a side note, we're having a little trouble with Bighorn Brewery and our liquor agreement with them. I wanted to talk to you about that while you're here. I hope I'm not interrupting." She paused just long enough to give Branson a chance to open his mouth to protest before launching into some explanation.

I sank back into my chair, taking some relief at the intrusion.

What was my problem? It wasn't like I was new to this. I'd already done the dating game; I'd been married. Granted, I was divorced for enough years that I was a little rusty; rusty enough that I probably matched the color of my hair, but not so much that I didn't remember how it went.

Maybe I was playing the part of the fool. From the moment I met Branson, he did something to me. Then again, I doubted there was a woman alive who wouldn't have experienced the same thing. The man was stunning. Stereotypical gorgeous, all-American man. The quintessential tall, dark, and handsome. Though he had plenty of power in his role on the police force, he was kind, helpful, funny, and... patient.

He really had been so patient. Never pressuring me more than I could handle, simply letting me know he was interested and waiting for me to say yes to our first date, then waiting for the next one and the next one.

I kept waiting for it to get easier, more natural—chalking it up to simply not being ready or prepared. I'd moved to Estes Park to hit reset on every area of my life, but not *that* particular area. I was done with men. I was done with romance. And within a hot second of moving to town, I had two beautiful men pining for my attention. Somehow, eight months later, here I was at a fancy bed-and-breakfast with the police sergeant, thinking I was about to receive a proposal.

I knew I didn't want that. I'd be insane to want that at this point. But did I want the rest?

I should. I knew I should. Branson's good qualities were nearly endless, and he made me nervous in a rather wonderful and exciting way.

What in the world was wrong with me?

As Meisel Pepper continued laying out her litany of concerns to Branson, I let my gaze wander over the other diners in the softly lit restaurant, the candlelight flickering off the crystals and glass, and then I focused out the wall of windows. It was late enough in the evening that the sun had set, leaving only the slightest purple outline over the rugged mountains of Rocky Mountain National Park in the distance. Between their peaks and our table, Estes Park spread before us. The clustered lights of downtown twinkled like a landing strip from Elkhorn Avenue and then seemed to starburst out from there, covering the surrounding valley with scattered neighborhoods, houses, and businesses.

The sight helped me breathe easier.

It had only taken me seconds to truly fall in love with Estes Park once I moved from the Midwest. Only moments for it to feel like home, for me to be sure this was the place I would find myself once more, become the woman I thought I was always meant to be. It hadn't been easy and not necessarily simple, but it felt right.

I didn't need things to be simple or easy with Branson before we crossed that line, but I did need them to feel right. I looked back to the box that didn't hold an engagement ring only to find it gone.

Suddenly I realized Ms. Pepper was gone as well and Branson was staring at me. This time, his smile seemed a little forced. "Sorry about that. Talk about a way to ruin the mood."

"It's okay. Part of the job. I understand that."

Branson returned to his prime rib. "You looked captivated by the view. It's spectacular, right?"

Apparently, we were simply going to move on. That worked for me. Though I knew we'd have to talk about it later. We were eating in a bed-and-breakfast. I supposed that would come sooner rather than later. But I took the reprieve that was offered. "Spectacular is the right word. I don't think I'll ever get tired of this place. I love that Estes will always be what it is. Being locked in on all sides with mountains, there's only so big it can grow, especially with so much of it being taken up by the national park."

Branson nodded his agreement as he sipped his wine but didn't offer any commentary. Maybe he could tell how strongly I was avoiding other conversations.

And I was. Somewhat desperately, but another topic entered my mind, and I latched on to it, focusing on him once more. "Mom told me that Officer Jackson went back to work full-time today."

His shoulders relaxed, and his smile became more genuine. "He did. Got a hero's welcome too."

"He should. He nearly died trying to protect Katie and me and Watson." Brent Jackson had gotten shot in the head four months earlier by a couple who'd been determined to kill Katie.

"The doctors say it's a miracle he survived, let alone that he made a full recovery." Branson's gaze darkened, and his tone grew serious. "I still feel horrible that I wasn't there when you needed me. I told you when we met I'd always keep you safe, and I failed."

The sincere guilt in his voice cut through me and warmed my heart. This time, I reached across the table and took his hand. "No, you didn't. You said I'd always be safe *with* you. And it was actually a promise you made to Watson to make him stop growling." I chuckled at the memory and was pleased to see a smile form on Branson's lips. "And as you may have noticed, I do just fine taking care of myself. Even as a police officer, you can't be there for people every hour of every day. You have nothing to apologize for."

He studied me in silence for a little while, and the ease grew between us again, more so than it had been all evening. When he finally spoke and didn't return to the conversation of rings or romance, I relaxed fully back into the moment. "Speaking of Estes never changing, I noticed the outside of Zelda and Verona's store is nearly done."

"Yeah. It looks nice. I have to admit, I was rather surprised with how simple they went with the recon-struction. It blends nicely with the Cozy Corgi. Now to see if Noah and Jonah go in a similar direction."

He cocked his head. "They're redoing the outside of their store too? It wasn't destroyed."

"Well, seeing the girls' store being revamped I think inspired them. They're in talks with Barry about redoing their property as well." A different kind of stress and worry arrived at the new topic, but it was much preferable to what had been there before. "It's funny how life works. If I'd been told that within a year I'd have my twin stepsisters opening a new age shop on one side of me and their twin husbands opening their inventor store on the other, I probably would've gone the other direction and seen what the East Coast had to offer." I laughed and felt oddly content. "I'm glad I didn't know. I would've hated to miss all of this."

"I'm glad you didn't know too." He gave another of his heart-stoppingly stunning smiles. "I would've hated to have missed you."

The rest of dinner went smoothly. We got lost in the gossip of the town and traded stories about silly tourists and shared an array of desserts that nearly rivaled the things Katie created.

The ease remained until Branson took my hand as we walked out of the restaurant. "Walk with me?" He motioned to the winding path that led down the slope in front of Pinecone Manor

"Sure."

We meandered in silence for several minutes. And though the tension built between us, both of us knowing that decisions would need to be made soon, it was also pleasant. The path was bordered by fairy lights that led us between massive pines, aspens, and boulders, some of which were spotlit here and there. Through the breaks in the trees, the glittering Valley of Estes and the darkening horizon of the mountains still shone through. Above, the crystalline Colorado sky covered us with the swirls and clusters of stars of the Milky Way.

Maybe I wasn't new to all of this, but the moment had the distinction of being the most beautiful and most romantic of my entire life. I couldn't imagine anything better.

We paused at a break in the trees. Branson slipped his arm around me, pulling me to his side gently, and we just stood, staring out at the lights and listening to the rustle of the gentle summer night breeze through the quaking aspen leaves. Occasionally, the peaceful silence was broken by the cry of a coyote or hoot of an owl.

After a while, with his free hand, Branson retrieved the box once more and held it out to me. "It's not a ring. And there are no expectations. It's just a token to show how much I care about you."

This time, the buzz in my blood and the nerves that came along with the box were rather pleasant. More like the flutter of butterflies as opposed to the spike of panic. I took the velvet box from his hand and lifted the lid.

A gold chain glittered inside, but it was dim enough that I had to lift it free before I could make out the details. A small pendant gleamed in the moonlight. I sucked in a pleased breath when I made out the details. It was a flat book, open so the pages curved out on either side, and in the middle was a cutout of a corgi.

"I got it at Aspen Gold, downtown. Like I said, I picked it out for your birthday, but they had to customize the corgi, and they took a ridiculously exorbitant amount of time." His voice was soft, and to my surprise, I realized he was nervous.

"I love it. And Watson would most definitely approve." I never wore gold, ever. Always pewter or silver, but I really did love it. "Thank you, Branson. It's absolutely beautiful." I shifted so I could meet his eyes. Though he was over six foot, with my heels, we were nearly at eye level.

"You're welcome. I'm glad you like it." Again, those nerves, so out of place on such a handsome, confident man. "May I put it on you?"

"Of course." I'd left my hair down, so I reached behind to gather it in my hands to lift it out of the way as Branson fixed the chain around my neck and fastened the ends before letting it fall. "It looks beautiful on you." He didn't step away, instead, looking at the necklace and then slowly lifting his gaze to mine. "You're so beautiful, Fred." Tentatively his hand rose, as if asking for permission, and then caressed my cheek.

For the billionth time that night, my pulse began to race, but this time in heat and desire.

He moved in, just half a step closer, and then lowered his lips to mine.

It wasn't our first kiss, but it was the most weighted, the most romantic—canopied by the stars, surrounded by the beauty of the mountains.

Branson moved closer still, letting his body press against mine as he deepened the kiss. His hand stroked gently through my hair while his other found the small of my back and pulled me nearer yet.

This was the moment. This was the time when it would feel right.

I let myself get lost in his kiss. In the feel of his touch and the warm hardness of his body. Allowed myself to float away.

And... I almost did. Almost reached that fuzzy, hazy place of passion and love or whatever laying in the middle.

Almost.

This was the time it would feel right, but it didn't.

I broke the kiss and stepped back, not much, just enough to feel more in control. I met his eyes. "I'm not ready. Sorry. But I'm not ready."

Branson didn't try to hide his disappointment, but neither did he show even the slightest flash of irritation or annoyance. "That's okay. There's never a rush. Ever."

I searched his gaze in the moonlight and found he was sincere. After a second, I slid back against him. "Can we just stand here and look at the stars for a while?"

"Of course we can."

Though we resumed the position we'd had only moments before and I truly believed he wasn't offended or angry, something wouldn't click back into place. Not quite.

"Oh my goodness, Katie. I typically don't enjoy attending sporting events, but if these are part of the package, consider me a convert." I popped another of the hot candied nuts into my mouth. The first one had been a peanut, but this one was a cashew and was even more mouthwatering.

"I'm glad you like them." Katie leaned over from where she sat on the other side of Leo Lopez on the bleachers, her brown spiraled hair bobbing to frame her round face. "With Nick working at the bakery, I have so much more time to experiment. I figured I'd try my hand at these this morning. Candied mixed nuts are better than the salted peanuts they have here I'm sure."

I plucked another from the white paper bag, this time a pecan. "Time well spent." I chewed on the nut while watching as the two softball teams traded places on the field. "Nick is a lifesaver, as is Ben. That boy really knows his books, but I think I might leave before the game is over, just go back and make sure they're doing okay. It doesn't seem fair to leave them alone on the busiest day of the year."

Leo, who had one arm flung easily over Katie's shoulders patted my knee. "Don't worry so much. The twins are doing great. I don't know how many times you made sure they both had yours and Katie's cell phone numbers before we left the Cozy Corgi. How many murders do you think can happen in your bookshop in less than a year?"

"Don't jinx us!" I shook my finger at him.

A crack sounded, pulling our attention to the field, and half the crowd filling the bleachers cheered. With the bases loaded, Mark Green tore off from home plate with surprising speed, considering his large size. He made it to first, then second before a red-haired woman on the other team, who looked more like a centerfold than an athlete, managed to retrieve the ball and throw it to one of her teammates. By the time Mark completed his homerun, his police officer sister, Susan, Paulie, and Melody, the woman I'd met at the pet shop a couple of days before, had all made it to home base as well.

Katie stood, both arms in the air as she jumped

up and down and screamed Paulie's name. Many in the crowd had the exact same reaction, causing the metal bleachers to sound like a thunderstorm.

Watson, who'd been napping in the shade beneath me, darted out from the lowest rung and glared in pure unadulterated offense.

"You're fine, little man, all is safe." Leo held out his hand toward Watson. "If looks could kill, every single one of us would be dead."

"Everybody but you." I shook my head as Watson forgot his annoyance and rushed like a long-lost lover to Leo's embrace. "I'd like to chalk it up to you just being a park ranger and good with animals, but I can't. My dog simply loves you more than me."

Ruffling Watson's fur, Leo looked over his shoulder and rolled his eyes. "You know that's not true. You're his entire world."

Leo was right. Watson had proved on more than one occasion that when it came down to it, I was the human he would choose time after time. "Maybe so, but he's a lot more demonstrative with you and my stepfather. Oh, and now Ben."

With a final pat on his head, Watson returned to his shady spot, and Leo leaned back once more. "Well, you can't blame him. That kid is a savant with animals. If he didn't love books and want to be a writer so badly, I'd try to steal him away. He could be the world's best park ranger."

"I got Ben first. Keep your hands off." I winked at him and leaned over so I could reach across and shove Katie's knee. "Maybe you can steal Nick. I thought I was gaining weight the way it was, but now that Katie has time to experiment, I never stop eating."

"Over my dead body. That boy is a godsend." Katie paused while the crowd cheered again, looked out at the softball field, and narrowed her eyes. "I can make out the emblems on most of the players shirts, but what in the world is on Susan's?"

I followed her gaze. Paulie's team, the Merchants, all wore neon yellow, but as one of their team members was Joe Singer who owned the T-shirt shop, it wasn't surprising that each one had a custom design on the front. "I can't tell."

"It's the ship from *The Love Boat.*"

Katie and I both turned to stare at Leo.

"I'm with you. All the other's made sense. But not in a million years would I have dreamed Susan Green was a closet *Love Boat* fan."

"Apparently, *not* so closeted." I watched as she ran across the field, and this time I could make it out. How strange. Everyone else had an emblem of something they clearly loved the most. Paulie's shirt had Ursula from *The Little Mermaid*, two eels, Flotsam and Jetsam flanking her on either side. Rion Sparks, who owned the wedding dress shop, had a wedding cake on his T-shirt, while Pete Miller had the logo for Hot Air, his glassblowing shop. Melody and the handsome man I assumed was her husband sported large, fluffy heads of Persian cats on their shirts. Even Susan's brother, who owned the magic shop, made sense with Harry Potter's lightning bolt on his chest. But with Susan, who was gruff, abrasive, and generally unpleasant, I would've expected a police baton, handcuffs, or a shotgun. Not *The Love Boat*, not in a million years.

Before the team switched sides again, the umpire announced a five-minute break. Most of the crowd got up to use the restroom or get snacks. The softball game was held at the high school, and some of the students were manning the concession stand, raising money for the senior trip. I would've felt guilty about Katie bringing in her candied nuts if the tickets to get into the game hadn't been twenty bucks apiece. Though really, whether a person was a softball fan or not, you couldn't ask for a more pleasant experience. The day was bright and pleasingly warm, and though the dark clouds gathering over the mountains seemed ominous, they added a rather beautiful effect in the background.

"So glad you're here, guys! Thank you so much for coming!" Paulie waved at us as he jogged by. We waved back and watched as he hurried over to where Flotsam and Jetsam were tied to a tree. I'd gone over a couple of times to check on them during the first few innings as the hyperactive dogs kept turning over their water. My presence only seemed to make them more insane.

Katie chuckled as she watched Paulie as well. He refilled the bowl and didn't even manage to get it placed on the ground before the tricolor corgi, Flotsam, knocked it out of Paulie's hands to lather him with kisses. "It's hard to believe that those two and Watson are the same breed."

I smiled over at her. "I'm pretty sure Watson would agree with you on that." I had to lean back to let someone pass on the bleachers, and as I readjusted, the sun shining on Melody's long blonde hair caught my attention. She looked deep in conversation with Pete Miller, his head bent toward her as if she was whispering. I scanned the rest of the field and saw her husband talking to Mark Green. For some reason, something seemed a little off, a little too intimate between Melody and a man who wasn't her husband. Maybe it was just my Midwest sensibilities raising their heads or looking for a story where there wasn't one. I lowered my voice to a whisper as I kept my gaze on Melody and Pete. "I met Melody the other day at Paulie's shop. I guess she and her husband moved to town a few months ago. As you can tell by their shirts, they're kind of obsessed with Persian cats."

Sure enough, as always in a small town, all it took was an innocuous statement to elicit more gossip. "I don't know her very well, but her husband is a really good guy. Jared took Declan's spot in the Feathered Friends Brigade after Henry was killed. Myrtle is still looking for two more members to take the other empty spots, if either of you have ten grand to spare."

Katie snorted.

Though I cast Leo a glance, I returned my focus to Melody and Pete. "Really? That seems odd for a guy who lives with seven cats. Aren't birds and cats mortal enemies?"

"A person can love cats *and* birds." Leo sounded unconcerned. "Jared's an animal lover."

Proving to be more on my wavelength, when Katie spoke, her tone seemed less convinced. "They've been into the bakery a couple of times. They are a really nice couple. Jared's the general manager of Bighorn Brewery, which is why they're on the Merchants team, but I heard that he has quite the temper."

"You know, I wouldn't put much stock in that." I shot her a wink. "I've heard that same rumor about a certain redhead who recently moved to town and opened a bookshop."

"What a coincidence, so have I." Katie returned the wink and cocked her head as she looked back at the field. "Well, look at that. There are more players in the game."

As we watched, the bombshell from the other team sashayed up to Pete and Melody. Before she arrived, Melody turned around and headed across the field toward her husband.

"That one lives up to the team name." There was a soft cackle behind me, and I turned to see an older Chinese woman, her poufy white hair gleaming in the afternoon sunlight.

"Petra. I didn't know you were here."

"Just arrived." She scowled and then flinched when she noticed Leo. "It seems I should've taken more time to locate a better place before I settled in."

"No need to move, Petra. We're good now, you and me." Leo smiled his handsome, good-natured smile and refocused on the field. Proving that he was more attuned to Katie and me than I thought, he didn't leave it at that. "And what do you mean? How does Delilah live up to the team name?"

For a moment, I thought Petra wasn't going to answer as she was silent for so long. She most definitely wasn't a fan of mine, but even though she, too, was part of the bird club, and Leo often led discussions for the group, when she'd been exposed for owning an endangered owl, she and Leo had been on different sides of the law.

Apparently, though, the gossip was too juicy to pass by, even if Petra didn't like Leo or me. "They're called the Cougars, aren't they? And Delilah Johnson is a cougar if I ever saw one."

"She hardly looks old enough to be qualified as a cougar."

"I thought you were supposed to be Little Miss Smarty-Pants." Petra offered another glower, this time to Katie. "She might spend half her profits from that photography store of hers on body enhancements, but she can't buy back years."

Katie didn't take the bait, instead gesturing toward the field. "Game's back on."

The Cougars were up at bat, and as chance had it, Delilah was up first. Paulie pitched the ball, and despite him not being able to pick up large bags of dog food on his own, he proved to have a strong arm. Even so, Delilah hit it with a loud crack and tore off toward first base.

I marveled at her; somehow, she even made that movement look alluring.

Before she quite reached it, Melody caught the ball, which had flown high, and got Delilah out.

"This is better than a soap opera." Behind us, Petra chuckled again. "That round went to the blonde bimbo with the stupid shirt."

"Petra!" I swiveled, looking at her, unable to keep the reproach out of my voice. "Melody is a very nice woman." I wasn't entirely sure if that was true or not, but she seemed nice enough, and Petra constantly rubbed me the wrong way.

Petra just glared, not bothering to reply.

"Plus," Katie jumped in, managing to keep her voice bright. "Melody's cat shirt actually makes a lot of sense. When softball was created in the 1880s, it was an inside sport for the first year, but the following season they moved it outside and dubbed it *kitten ball*. They named it that because Lewis Rober's team was called the Kittens." She stopped talking, then threw in a last detail, clearly unable to help herself. "He was a fireman."

Leo nearly shook with laughter, and Petra just stared.

I had a sneaking suspicion that my best friend had gone on one of her Google binges, knowing that we were coming to a softball game, and I was willing to bet she was close to bursting with wanting to share the hoard of factoids. I decided to help her out, though I wasn't certain if it was truly to play the role of best friend or to annoy Petra. I took a wild swing at it. "Is softball that popular a sport, Katie?"

She nodded enthusiastically, sending her curls dancing again and sure enough, sounded relieved. "It's actually the number one sport in America. Over forty million people play it."

Petra huffed. "You're a strange, freaky bird, Katie Pizzolato."

Katie lifted her chin. "While we're at it, you might find it interesting to know that in Chicago they use a larger sixteen-inch softball to represent the original one, which was simply a balled-up boxing glove they hit with the bat. That game is called mushball, and they're not allowed to use mitts; they have to catch it with their bare hands."

Leo finally lost it, threw back his head and nearly howled with laughter.

Katie swatted at him. "Hey, that's not very nice!"

Still laughing, he threw his arms around her and pulled her to him. "Come here, my little trivia freak."

Though I joined in the laughter, I couldn't keep from wondering, not for the first time, if there was more than friendship between Katie and Leo. It sure looked that way.

There was a shuffling behind us. "Talk about wallowing in the riffraff. I'm going to go find better seats,"

As Petra huffed away, Leo was taken up in laughter once again.

It was cut short by screamed curses. The three of us whipped back toward the field just in time to see Jared Pitts throw his glove to the ground, rush at Pete Miller, and take him down in what looked like a painful tackle.

Everyone in the bleachers stood at once, causing Watson to dart back out again. Within moments, other members of the team had pulled Jared and Pete apart.

"Well...." Katie let out a long breath as we sat back down. "I'd heard he had a temper."

Before the game could resume, the storm clouds previously over the mountains had traveled without my noticing. With a loud crack of thunder, they opened and gave in to the daily afternoon rainstorm.

FOUR

Watson lay at Barry's feet, his large brown eyes darting constantly back and forth, one minute with a look of adoration at my stepfather, the next clearly debating if the entire spread of food over the eight large blankets was there for his enjoyment.

"The Fourth of July is my absolute favorite holiday." Barry stood with his hands on his hips in Peter Pan fashion as he looked over the feast. "With a few exceptions, it has the most vegetarian-friendly options of them all."

"Which is surprising, considering it's a holiday revolving around war and celebrated with shooting fire up in the air. The whole thing is the epitome of straight men compensating for something." Percival shook a large turkey leg toward the concession stands on the far side of the open space. "And there are plenty of meat options available over there for those of us who are actual red-blooded men."

"Now who's compensating?" His husband, Gary, patted Percival's knee in a mock soothing manner, eliciting a scowl.

Mom jumped in, clearly hoping to distract her brother before he and Gary got into a snit. "Besides, Percival, I think the fireworks would be right up your alley. They're so sparkly and flamboyant."

"Flamboyant? Baby girl, I am *not* flamboyant." Percival sniffed, and tilted his chin regally. "I simply have elevated tastes."

"The red, white, and blue sequins covering your vest would say otherwise." Barry grinned, clearly teasing, but then his eyes narrowed at the giant turkey leg. "And remind me to show you videos of how the birds are treated on poultry farms."

"Sequins?" Percival sucked in a shocked gasp as he shimmied in his vest, causing the light of the dipping sun to scatter red, white, and blue fractals around the picnic. "These are rhinestones, you peasant." Once more he used the turkey leg as a pointing device, this time zigzagging it as he encompassed the entirety of Barry's body. Flecks of meat flew off, causing Watson moments of joy as he scampered and devoured. "You're    hardly    one    to    talk    about wardrobes and fashion choices. Tell me, where does one acquire a tie-dyed jumpsuit? Or did it come free with purchase when you spend one hundred dollars or more at Hippies "R" Us?"

"We really should be live-streaming this on YouTube." Leo grinned over at Katie and me from where the three of us were seated on the edge of the blankets. "We could get them a sitcom within a week. We'll call it *Keeping Up with the Octogenarians.*"

Katie didn't take her gaze away from the foursome. "Nobody would believe it wasn't scripted. They'd call it too over the top."

I elbowed Leo playfully. "Keep your voice lower. If Percival hears you call him an octogenarian, he's liable to kill you with that turkey leg. He keeps trying to convince people he's the same age as Gary, a young spry man in his sixties. Heaven forbid you add on an extra decade." I shook my head, still marveling at how my life had changed from growing up in Kansas City with just my mother and father. "Plus, if you're really going to live-stream it, you might as well wait until Verona's and Zelda's clan gets here. Really get the *whole* family in action."

We settled in, content to watch the shenanigans.

Pure contentment washed over me. Life was good, so very, very good.

As I glanced around, I realized our little scene was played out over and over again throughout the area. Probably not as ridiculous in many ways as my family, but who knew? The entire town had arrived, spreading their blankets over the wide-open space of the fairgrounds that bordered Lake Estes. Not only the whole town, but hundreds upon hundreds of tourists, probably thousands. People had said that there wasn't a better place to watch a firework display than Estes Park. I hadn't seen one there since I'd been a child, but at that point, one firework show looked like another. But now I could truly appreciate it—the perfection of the mountains encircling us on all sides, the huge, deep blue Colorado sky, the crystalline lake, the fresh mountain air smelling of pine... even a small herd of female elk with their gangly calves wandering on the far edge of the festivities, not concerned about the hordes of people.

After all the upheaval in my life that had caused me to hit reset the previous fall, I'd gone and landed in paradise.

Within half an hour, Barry's twin daughters, Zelda and Verona, their twin husbands, Noah and Jonah, and their four children arrived, filling up the rest of the space on the blankets both with their bodies and more food.

It took less than a minute for Watson to decide that there were too many feet, too many hands, and entirely too many voices before he sauntered over and curled up at Leo's side.

"See?" I reached over and scratched Watson's ear, earning myself a sidelong glance. "With you and Barry around, I'm chopped liver."

Leo grinned. "If there was actually chopped liver, I'm pretty sure Watson wouldn't be concerned with any of us."

"Actually, I came armed with a weapon." Katie twisted so she could dig in her purse before turning back around and holding something in front of her. "Oh, Watson."

Though it took him several moments, Watson finally deigned to turn his attention to Katie, and his eyes went wide.

"That's right! Who has your favorite all-natural snack?" She waggled the large bone-shaped treat and was rewarded with a thirty-three-pound corgi-shaped bullet in her lap. After regaining her balance, she leered at Leo. "Who's the favorite now?"

Watson had barely taken his first bite when his ears perked, and he sat up, eyes panicked.

Feeling a jolt of alarm, I followed his gaze and then laughed and gave a wave. "You're welcome to join us!"

Paulie was several yards away, struggling with a large picnic basket in one hand and his two insane corgis pulling in opposite directions on their leashes that he held in his other hand. Beside him, Athena Rose, the obituary writer for *The Chipmunk Chronicles*, carried a smaller picnic basket and a large purse with a white teacup poodle poking her head over the top.

Athena noticed me first, gave a wave, and then motioned in our direction to Paulie.

"You sure you don't mind if we join you?" Paulie was breathless when he reached us, his eyes strained and bloodshot.

"No. Of course not." I gestured toward the mounds of food. "We've got more than enough to share."

Athena smiled and glanced at Katie. "Please tell me that's your strawberry shortcake I see."

"Sure is." Katie beamed. Athena was also a food blogger and the object of Katie's hero-worship.

"Well, I'm sold!" Athena set down her basket in a graceful manner that I envied. Athena always looked so put together, like a sophisticated older

African-American model just traveling from Milan or Paris. I didn't know how she managed it.

"Please take these two." Paulie thrust Flotsam and Jetsam toward Leo. "One more minute and I think I'd murder them."

Leo took them instantly but had to stand in order to avoid being dragged toward the food.

"Are you okay?" Katie stood as well, helping Paulie untangle himself from the picnic basket.

"Yes. It's been a long afternoon." His smile seemed forced, and though his gaze flitted over us, he didn't meet anyone's eyes. "Just tired from the softball game is all."

I'd seen Paulie sad many times, and lonely. And truth be told, he was always a little strange, though that aspect was growing more endearing by the day, but I'd never seen him like this, whatever it was— flustered, angry, almost... afraid... maybe.

"Paulie! Athena!" Mom hurried over, giving both of them hugs, and then within a few minutes, our little mishmash of friends and family began to feast.

Once more, I was struck by how different my life was suddenly, and how we weren't exactly a little group. Not counting the four dogs, there were sixteen of us spread over those eight blankets. And again, life was good.

Food had been devoured by the time the sun was nearly tucked behind the mountain peaks, and the firework display was getting closer and closer. The four kids had just returned from playing with friends at the playground by the concession stands, my step-sisters and their husbands talked over their store renovation plans with Barry, and Percival and the rest of us lounged, chatting quietly as we continued to pick at the remaining smorgasbord of desserts. Even Flotsam and Jetsam had worn themselves out and were now asleep in a mud puddle that had been formed when one of the kids knocked over the pitcher of iced tea.

At my feet, Watson and Pearl, Athena's teacup poodle, snuggled together in dreams.

"They're so cute." Athena smiled down at the two before glancing my way. "I'm pretty sure if Pearl had a diary, she'd be writing Watson's name inside little hearts every night."

"I'd say you're right." I slipped out my cell phone and snapped a picture of the two. "Watson even shared his favorite dog treat with her. For a normal person, that would be like taking a bullet."

She chuckled. "Well, Katie did say it was his third one."

"Oh no!" Katie shook her head. "Trust me, it wouldn't matter if it was his fiftieth; Watson does *not* share his treats."

"Or anything else, for that matter." I snapped another picture for good measure. "I never dreamed my little man would have a girlfriend."

"Speaking of girlfriends...." Percival piped in with a singsong voice. "Or *boy*friends, rather. Isn't that yours coming this way, Fred?" He pointed behind my back.

I turned and spotted Branson wearing his police uniform, sitting atop a chestnut-brown horse with a long black mane. They were carefully meandering through the crowds of picnickers.

Nearby, Athena issued a low growl that contrasted with her flawlessly elegant appearance. "Hmmm-hmmm, gotta love a man in uniform. Especially when they look like that."

"I'll say!" Katie and Percival spoke in unison and then laughed.

That moment, probably feeling our attention, Branson looked our way and caught my gaze.

He hesitated, probably not long enough for anyone else to notice, but I did. Felt the awkward strain, even at this distance. Things had ended pleasantly enough on our date, but though there'd been a couple of text messages, there'd been no real communication since. The tension was gone in a flash, and with his movie-star smile in place, he pulled on the reins of his horse and headed our way.

"How are you all doing tonight?" Branson slid off the horse when he reached our blankets.

"Better now!" Percival practically purred.

Gary smacked him on the shoulder though he chuckled.

Branson gave an indulgent smile their way, which faded as he noticed Leo. "Thought you'd be looking for poachers this evening. Isn't Fourth of July supposed to be a big night for that? With all the distractions of fireworks and such?"

I knew the two of them had had a rocky past, but I hadn't heard Branson use such a taunting tone with Leo before.

"The last few times we've tried to get the police involved, I believe the official response was that we were overreacting." Leo's voice was cold and emotionless, a sound I'd never heard from him, either. "Figured I might as well take a night off."

Before Leo could respond, Paulie nearly

squeaked. "Would your horse like an apple... or something, Sergeant Wexler?"

"No, thank you. He's fine."

Branson held his gaze on Leo for several heartbeats before looking past Paulie to me. "Fred. Good to see you."

The whole interaction was throwing me off, I felt like I was several pages behind. Or maybe in the wrong book entirely. "You too." It seemed we were going to be formal.

"You know, while you're here...." Barry rushed over, his cheerful tone revealing he was oblivious to the tension that had fallen over everyone else. "We haven't had a family picture in ages, not with all of us together. And there's just enough light left." He thrust his cell phone toward Branson. "Would you mind?"

Almost looking relieved at the break, Branson nodded. "Of course."

Without waiting a second, Barry whirled and began orchestrating where everyone should stand. "Fred, try that patriotic top hat on Watson again. Maybe with his girlfriend around, he'll oblige. It would be super cute for the photo."

Paulie moved away, gathering up Flotsam and

Jetsam's leashes. "Come on, boys. Let's get out of the way."

I grabbed his hand. "No, be in it with us. Please."

His eyes widened, and for the first time since he'd arrived, the look of the stress, hurt, or whatever it was, left. "Really?"

"Of course!" I gave his hand a squeeze and then turned toward Leo, Katie, and Athena. "All of you. I insist."

"So do I." Mom appeared at Katie's side and slipped one of her birdlike arms around her. "We're all family here."

Sounding like himself again, Paulie chirped. "Wonderful. I brought the hats I got for the boys with me, just in case. Give me a minute." He waggled a hand at Athena. "Put on Pearl's too."

By the time we were all arranged, there was barely any light left, but Barry had been right. Though I wasn't sure if it was because Pearl was watching or that I'd asked Leo to put the hat on, but Watson made no other protest than a solid expression at having the top hat tied onto his head. Beside him, Pearl had on a bejeweled tiara that didn't seem to have anything to do with Fourth of July but still fit her perfectly.

Branson mounted his horse once more to get a

better angle for the picture, and everyone smiled. Everyone except for Watson, who continued to scowl, and Flotsam and Jetsam who, though they kept their Betsy Ross and Statue of Liberty hats on, were captured in the game of trying to bite off each other's ears.

After five different attempts, Barry was finally satisfied with the results and took his camera back. Branson didn't get off his horse again, nor did he look at anyone else besides me. "I hope you enjoy the rest of your evening, Fred. Happy Fourth."

"Happy Fourth, Branson."

He was gone before I could say anything more.

Katie gave me a look that clearly stated, *What in the world was that?*

I shrugged and turned away before she could ask. I'd sugarcoated the date's events when I'd filled her in after. They felt too private and not clearly understood. Maybe if I'd talked them over with my best friend, I would've understood them a little bit more, but I hadn't. And with the way things had just gone with Branson, I was even more confused. And a touch sad, like something was slipping through my fingers. Well... not something. Obviously. Like *Branson* was slipping through my fingers.

By the time darkness settled in and the stars glittered in the sky, our large group was gathered in a pleasantly warm bundle of blankets, people, and puppies, against the cool Colorado breeze.

All thoughts of Branson, curiosity about Paulie's stress, and any sense of melancholy vanished as the fireworks began and took my breath away.

It seemed I wasn't the only one. Though there were thousands of people spread out under the stars, not one voice broke through the night, all of us completely captured in wonder.

With every explosion of color, spark, and sizzle, the mountains were lit up, beautiful giants appearing in the dark and then gone again, and all the while the black mirrored surface of the lake echoed each burst of gold, silver, red, and blue.

Not only was life good, it was magic.

## FIVE

"See this spot right here?" Ben knelt, stroking the white diamond patch at the nape of Watson's neck.

The two children nodded.

Ben swept a lock of dark hair behind his ear, then returned to stroking Watson. "According to Welsh mythology, this is the fairy saddle."

The brother and sister's eyes grew larger, and their mother grinned over at me as Ben continued his lesson.

"The corgis would pull their chariots for royal processions and into battle." He then patted Watson's round belly splayed out on the floor. "Can you imagine this little guy being a fairy warrior?"

The little girl nodded enthusiastically, but her brother sounded skeptical. "Isn't he a little fat to be a warrior? I don't think he could run very fast."

"Then you should see him when he hears the

word T-R-E-A-T. He's like a racehorse." I couldn't
help but chuckle when the little boy scowled
at me.

His sister sucked in a quick gasp. "I know what
that spells! *Treat.* He runs when he hears the
word *treat*!"

Proving her correct, Watson popped up in a
clatter of claws on the hardwood floor of the
bookshop.

The children laughed and took a step back.

"See?" I reached behind the counter and pulled
out a treat the size of a chocolate chip. "If he can
move that quickly for a treat, imagine what he'd do
for a fairy." I tossed the morsel to Watson, and
though he caught it effortlessly, his disdain was obvious. Being the mascot of the Cozy Corgi meant he
got treats constantly, so we had to make an adjust-
ment, moving away from the more sizable dog bones
to the tiny little nuggets. At least for moments like
this. Despite him acting like a martyr, he still had
more elaborate and constant treats than any other
dog I'd ever met.

"You know where I learned about that?" Ben
waited until he had the kids' attention once more.
"In books. You can learn a lot of really cool things
from books."

"Do you have a book about corgis for kids?" It was like the little girl had a script.

"We're a bookstore called the Cozy Corgi. Of course we have books about corgis for kids." Ben stood and made a follow-me gesture. "Let me show you. There's a little couch in the kids' section where you can sit and read it. You don't even have to buy it."

The mother hung back for a second as her children followed Ben across the store. She gave me a knowing eyebrow raise and pointed at Ben's back, Watson trotting along happily at his feet. "You've got a goldmine with those two. Didn't see that sales pitch coming until it hit me in the face."

I felt my cheeks burn. "He was serious. There's no pressure to buy the book. They just sit there and read as long as you want."

"You don't have children, do you?" She barely gave me time to shake my head. "There's no child alive that's going to hear a fairytale about a dog that's right in front of them, then see the book, and not throw the holy terror of tantrums if their parent doesn't buy it for them." She winked good-naturedly. "Well played."

I chewed my bottom lip as I watched her go, feeling guilty. If she did buy it, I'd give a discount.

She wasn't wrong. Ben was a goldmine. Not only was he the equivalent of catnip for every animal that crossed his path, but he had the exact same effect on children. And with his sweet, quiet nature, most mothers responded just like that one. He was too charming to inspire irritation. In the time that he'd worked at the bookshop, I'd had to restock the kids' section multiple times. I was going to have to talk to him about being a little subtler, however.

Maybe...

The day after the Fourth of July had proven nearly as busy as the holiday itself. Though I didn't know how they'd pulled it off, Ben and Nick had done a stellar job running the bakery and bookstore through the afternoon. Katie and I had already decided we were going to give them raises. It was barely three o'clock, and my feet ached from all the running around with customers and that was *with* Ben's help. I hadn't even had a moment to read a few chapters in my favorite spot in the mystery room. And we'd been so busy that Katie hadn't made an appearance from the bakery since breakfast. I had no idea how the twins had managed the day before.

Within a minute or two, Watson waddled back over and gave me an expectant look.

"Dream on, buddy. I appreciate you not eating

the children, but no more morsels for a while." I bent down to pet his head.

With a chuff, he ducked, avoiding my hand, and continued his journey across the store to plop down in front of the window to nap. Unfortunately for him, there was no sunshine in his favorite spot since the day had been unusually rainy. I was going to have to make sure to give the floors a good mopping at the end of the day to avoid any water damage from all the wet traffic.

Strangely, there was a break in the tourists that offered me a second to myself. I glanced toward the mystery room, my newest London Lovett novel calling to me. There was nothing like curling up with a book on a rainy day. But I knew no sooner would I get situated than another customer would come in. Instead I decided to act like the professional I was and started sifting through the mail that had been delivered that morning.

I made piles of bills, advertisements that were of interest, and junk. Luckily, the junk pile grew much quicker than the one of bills. Near the bottom of the stack, a pale pink card stock oval with scalloped edges caught my attention and I pulled it free.

For a second, I wasn't certain what I was looking at. In the center was a picture of two Persian kittens, and above them in a white font fit for royalty, British or fairy, read *Introducing Belvedere & Cameo*.

It wasn't until I turned the card over and saw a smiling image of Melody and Jared Pitts, sitting on a sofa surrounded by their seven cats, that I clued in. Below the image, read:

*We're pleased to announce that Belvedere and Cameo will be joining our little family when they are old enough next month. In honor of their soon-to-be arrival, we want to celebrate. Join us in our happiness by using this card to get a free craft beer from Bighorn Brewery and a ten percent discount on any Merchants merchandise from Rocky Mountain Imprints. Feel free to drop by our home to meet our new sweet babies soon, or we will see you at the brewery or at one of the games.*

*With love, Angel, Beatrice, Cinnamon, Ethel, Finnegan, Leroy, Sherbet, Melody and Jared*

Every once in a while, I worried I'd become the crazy corgi lady. As I stared at the announcement and coupon combo, that fear vanished. At least by comparison to the crazy cat people, I was the picture of sanity.

A loud crack of thunder rumbled through the store, and there was a sharp scream from up in the bakery, followed by a laugh. Outside the windows, the summer shower became a downpour. Tourists rushed to the doorway, some of them coming into the shop, others simply taking refuge under the awning.

Ben appeared at my shoulder and looked at the announcement. "Are you getting a cat?"

"Not hardly." I laughed. "I'm fairly certain Watson would murder me if I brought home another corgi. It would be an all-out torture session if I tried to bring in a cat. It seems—"

There were loud gasps by the windows, and Ben and I both looked over. For a few seconds, I didn't see what caused the commotion. When I did, I sucked in a gasp of my own. Beside me, I heard Ben issue the same response.

Without speaking, he and I both walked from behind the counter, joining the crowd at the window. Luckily, we were both tall enough that we could see easily.

Outside, not bothered in the least, a herd of seven or eight bull elk made their way along the streets, passing easily through the cars that had come to a standstill in their presence. Talk about royalty. I loved my little corgi, but if you were going to choose an animal to ride into battle, those were the way to go. With their spiked crowns of antlers sparkling in the glistening rain, they truly did look ethereal.

It wasn't the first time elk had wandered through downtown, nor would it be the last. A week ago, there'd been a mountain lion in a tree outside my uncles' antique shop, and almost every week someone stumbled upon a black bear rummaging through the dumpsters behind the stores. But with the ferocity of the thunder and lightning, and the way the herd of animals held their heads aloft as rain poured over their hides, the moment truly was breathtaking.

And I got to live in a place like Estes Park where things like this happened. Not only live there but have my dream bookshop and be surrounded by friends and family. How lucky was I? "I can't believe this is my life."

"Pretty great, huh?"

At his whisper, I spared Ben a glance as he stared out the window, enraptured like everyone else. I hadn't realized I'd spoken aloud. "Yeah, it is. Pretty great."


Five minutes later, the elk were gone, traffic was moving again, the rain was nothing more than a mist, and the tourists resumed their meandering along the sidewalks. With the exception of the bakery, the store was empty. I motioned across the street with my chin as I addressed Ben. "I got a message from Paulie at lunch letting me know an item I ordered the other day came in." I lowered my voice. "It's another hat. Headband, really, but it has a stack of three foam books on top. I'm going to find a way to do a little photo shoot of Watson wearing it. It will be great for advertisements and newsletters."

"Weren't you just saying something about him murdering you?" Though Ben was still quiet and shy, he'd opened up a lot over the past weeks, even teasing every so often, clearly comfortable around me and in the bookshop. It was nice to see. He, and his brother, for that matter, seemed to carry so much sadness around with them, but they seemed lighter somehow.

"I think it will be cute enough that it'll be worth me taking my chances." I swirled my finger in the air, encompassing the store. "You good on your own for a few minutes?" He opened his mouth to respond, but I cut him off. "Never mind, of course you are. You handled the store yesterday, and it was a madhouse." He'd just graduated high school at the end of May. I needed to not treat him like a kid. "I'll be right back."

I slipped into my raincoat and headed toward the door. Watson woke and trotted over to me. Pausing with my hand on the doorknob, I looked down at him. "You can stay here. I'll be quick."

He whined.

With a shrug I retrieved his leash. "Well, I tried to warn you."

As we crossed the street and approached the door of Paws, Watson gave me a betrayed look.

"Oh please, you can't blame me for this." I opened the door and stood out of the way to let Watson sulk in before me. Both of us instantly froze in place, Flotsam and Jetsam's barking nearly an assault on our ears.

Again, Watson whined. That time, I couldn't blame him.

The pet shop was never quiet, but at the moment, it was beyond a cacophony of noises. Much more than I'd ever heard, and not just the corgis. Parrots and other birds screeched and squawked at a horrible decibel. It even seemed like the metallic whirl of rodent wheels was more frantic than normal.

The cat castle had been moved to the center of the store. A huge blue bow was affixed to the tallest turret with a large green tag that read *To Jared* written in flowery script surrounded by bubble-like hearts.

Beyond that, there was no one; the store seemed empty.

"Paulie?" At my raised voice, Watson jumped, and the parrots screeched louder. A second later, barking wild and vicious, Flotsam and Jetsam tore through the store, crashing into each other as they rounded the corner and ran at us. From their flashing fangs I could see why the fairies might have chosen to ride them into battle after all.

Watson stood in front of me, head lowered, lips curled and gave a warning growl.

To my surprise, Flotsam and Jetsam slowed, and their aggressive sounds turned to pitiful whines and cries.

I had no idea Watson had that power. I wondered if he'd realized. Surely he would've used it before then if he had.

Still whining, Flotsam rolled over to expose his belly, and Jetsam kept looking over his shoulder and barking.

"What's wrong, boys?" Cold ice seemed to pour over me. Paulie wasn't answering, and there was no doubt from the dogs' behavior that something was truly wrong. Maybe Paulie had tried to move the dog food on his own, knocked several bags over and was buried under them or something. Not wasting another second, I hurried through the store, heading around the counter.

Just as I did, something crunched beneath my feet.

I glanced down and saw the crumpled announcement of Belvedere and Cameo. I started to take another step, and then noticed the pool of blood a few inches away

Again, Watson growled, and Flotsam and Jetsam whimpered.

Melody Pitts lay on the floor, partially hidden behind the counter. Her blonde hair splayed over blood on the floor, her blue eyes glassy, and a pair of scissor handles protruded from her throat.

"Oh my...." I took a step back, lifting my fingers to my lips. Though I'd seen multiple dead bodies since moving to town, I'd been utterly and completely unprepared for the sight in that moment, and it took a couple of heartbeats for my brain to clear. "Branson. I need to call Branson."

Flotsam and Jetsam started barking again and were jumping up and down on their forepaws several feet away.

"I know, boys. I know." I dug in the pocket of my skirt to get my phone but froze once more as Watson walked to the other two corgis, his head down, his lips curled once more, then went past them. As he reached the door that led to the back room, he paused and growled, sounding more dangerous than I'd ever heard him.

I rushed toward him, realizing what he'd seen. I hadn't expected to find Melody, which meant that Paulie still had to be there somewhere.

Sure enough, I saw him the second I hurried into the room. Calling out his name, I rushed to his side. Paulie lay on the ground in his own pool of blood near the back door. His thin, pale hand atop a wound in his side.

Forgetting protocol in a way that should shame a policeman's daughter, I knelt beside him, not worried about prints or evidence. "Paulie, oh... Paulie."

Through the blur of my tears, I noticed a slight rise of his chest.

I wiped my tears away and blinked.

"You're alive!" In my relief, I must've lost my sanity as I nearly bent down to hug him. Catching myself, I retrieved my phone and dialed 911.

As it rang, I pressed my fingers under his throat. His pulse was weak, barely there. Only then did I notice another wound on the side of his head, as if he'd been hit with something.

"911, what is your emergency?"

Before I could answer, there was a horrid, gut-wrenching cry from the other room.

Nearly slipping, I stood and ran back to the doorway, where I found Jared Pitts kneeling on the floor, holding his wife's body to his chest, and wailing.

We were the only four in the hospital waiting room—
Katie, Leo, Athena, and me. Well, five counting
Pearl, who poked her head up out of Athena's purse
every so often to survey the room but then curled
back down, returning to her nap. I'd taken the time
between the pet shop and the hospital to run Watson
to my house, knowing the hospital would frown on a
dog in the waiting room. I wished I hadn't. Pearl's
presence was a comfort, but Watson's would've been
preferable. Although, I was certain Athena Rose
could get away with things that I never could. Even
if she was almost half my size, Athena could stop a
charging bull elephant with a cocked eyebrow. I was
certain if the nurse at the front desk had started to
protest at the sight of the little teacup poodle, all it
would have taken was a withering glance to leave her
a puddle in her chair.

"How much longer til an update? They haven't told us anything." Katie wrung her hands as she paced, her puffy, red-rimmed eyes confirming that Paulie really had worked his way into our circle of friendship.

"Technically, they don't have to update us at all. None of us are Paulie's family." Though seated, Leo's leg shook nervously in time with Katie's steps.

Athena scoffed. "I'd like to see them try to pull that. We're the closest thing to family he probably has here. Plus, I know Dr. William's mother. Gladys and I go on monthly shopping trips to the city. That boy knows better than to cross me."

I couldn't bring myself to chime in. I kept seeing Paulie lying there on the floor of his storeroom, so pale. The others couldn't grasp how close Paulie had been to death, but I did. I'd been certain from the looks of him, from the stab wound in his side. And when the paramedics had put him on the stretcher... his head injury was so much worse than I'd realized.

"Did you know there are a hundred billion neurons in our brain? That's the same number of stars in the Milky Way." Katie continued to pace, but she seemed to be on the same wavelength as me, kinda. "Isn't that amazing? Just think of all the stars we saw last night before the fireworks. That vast amount of beauty is inside each of our heads."

"Yeah. It's pretty awesome." Though his voice was soft, Leo smiled indulgently at her.

Katie just kept walking back and forth between the door and the window overlooking the parking lot. "The brain doesn't have any pain receptors. Doctors can actually perform surgery on it without putting a patient under. Of course, they'd feel the cutting of the skull and things—"

"I'm going to stop you there." Athena paired her raised eyebrow with a hand. "That's not something I want to be thinking about right now."

Katie blushed, paced a few more steps, and sat down between Leo and me. "I wish they'd tell us *something*. I just don't understand. Who in the world would want to hurt Paulie?" Her blush deepened. "Oh goodness, I don't mean it like that. I don't know who would want to hurt Melody either..."

Leo patted her knee. "It's okay. None of us took it like that. It only makes sense that Paulie is our first priority. We didn't know Melody very well, and she's beyond worry now. It's okay to give Paulie all of our focus."

Athena nodded. "Exactly right. He's one of ours. He's going to be okay. He's tougher than a person would think. Definitely tougher than I thought the first time I met that strange little man." She choked out an affectionate laugh, but her eyes remained dry.

"That is the question though, Katie." I latched on to the thought, desperate for something to take my mind off the worry. And to give myself something to do that might actually help. "Granted, I didn't get to spend much time looking at the shop, but it didn't look like a robbery. Someone went there specifically to hurt Paulie. But why? More importantly, who?"

Though they looked at me, the three of them were silent. After a few moments Katie spoke up, her voice brightening slightly. "Maybe that's it. Maybe nobody wanted to hurt Paulie. It was just like we said before, who would want to hurt him? He's a sweetheart, and harmless. It wouldn't surprise me if instead of giving dogs a flea bath, he'd pick off the little critters one by one and send them to some flea rescue organization or something."

The four of us chuckled at that idea. Though exaggerated, I could almost see Paulie doing something like that. It was Leo who disagreed with her, though. "But if Melody was the real target, why would it happen at Paws? Wouldn't they do it at her home or...." His brows furrowed. "Where does... *did*... Melody work?"

An exchange of glances revealed that none of us knew.

"I agree. I have to believe that Melody was just at the wrong place at the wrong time." Though she was the one who'd died, there was a more vicious feel to Paulie's injuries. But I wasn't going to say that. It felt disrespectful to Melody, to take away from the injustice of having scissors in her neck.

"Okay, that makes sense." Katie nodded, spiral curls bobbing. "But still... who would want to hurt Paulie? The only thing I can think of is if he sold rancid dog food or something by accident, or someone's cat choked on a toy. But if that had happened, Paulie would've felt horrible and been a mess. And he wasn't." She blinked, considering. "Although... he seemed a little stressed lately."

Her words triggered a thought that had been trying to form since the day before. "You're right. I noticed that at the firework display. He was so frustrated with Flotsam and Jetsam. I'd never seen him like that. Granted, I can't imagine anyone in their right mind not being frustrated with Flotsam and Jetsam, but Paulie always seemed like he was completely oblivious to their bad behavior and never even slightly annoyed."

"Yeah." Leo angled his head toward me slowly,

recollection dawning. "He even said he was close to murdering them. I know he was teasing, of course, but... yeah... you're right."

Athena was oddly quiet, and her silence drew my attention. Her lips were little more than a thin, tight line, and her focus was laser-sharp on Pearl who was poking her head out of her purse once more. Athena's greenish-brown eyes flicked at me from underneath her thick false eyelashes and quickly returned to Pearl.

She knew something. Jolts went through me at the realization. Both in surprise and in something like relief. There was more that I could do than sit here and worry about Paulie. I could figure something out. If Paulie woke up... no... *when* Paulie woke up. *When.* Maybe by the time he was conscious again, the person who'd harmed him would be put away, and he'd be safe.

"Athena?"

She didn't look up, just kept scratching Pearl's head with her french-tipped nails.

Beside me, Leo and Katie both focused on Athena as well, each sitting straighter as they came to attention.

"Athena, what are you thinking?"

She looked at me then, a slight challenge in her

gaze, but it only lasted for a heartbeat before she sighed and sank back into her chair, giving into atypical poor posture. "I feel like I'm betraying him, but I suppose that's silly. We're all on the same side. On Paulie's side."

The three of us nodded as if she were asking for confirmation.

Athena considered again, then nodded. "I don't know much. I just know that he hasn't been himself the past week or two. A little more on edge. And, you're right. He's been that way even with his boys; that's how I first noticed. But then a couple of days ago, I walked into the pet shop on my lunch break. The two of us had plans to go eat at Penelope's. I was craving a burger and a malt, and they have the best…. Never mind, that's not important." She waved her hand in the air. "Anyway. There was this mousy blonde-looking woman. I know that's not nice to say, but it's the best way to describe her, at least from the brief glance I got as she left the store. The two of them had been talking at the counter when I walked in, and it seemed like a rather intense conversation from their body language and the energy of the room. As soon as I arrived, the woman left. Instantly."

I waited a second, thinking there was more to

say, she just looked at me expectantly. "Athena, why would you feel like you're betraying Paulie by telling us that?"

"Because... I inquired about what was wrong. I thought maybe it was a customer making some demands about an exchange or who was unhappy with something. Expected some irritating yet funny story; you know how it can get during tourist season. Even at the newspaper it's unbelievable the things people come in asking for." She sighed, once more seeming like the words were being forced from her. "Paulie about bit my head off for asking. Then apologized instantly, of course. But made it very clear that we weren't going to talk about it. Then through the entire lunch he was overly cheerful, forced, you know? Something was wrong."

I quickly played through the details she'd given, feeling like I was missing something. Clearly it was a great place to start. It seemed too much of a coincidence for Paulie to act in a manner so atypical just a few days before he was attacked. "I still don't get why you'd feel the need to keep it a secret."

"You thought it was a lovers' spat." Katie's voice was soft, almost wistful.

I turned to her, confused by her tone.

"I did." Athena relaxed somewhat and focused

on Katie instead of me. "Though I hated that they were arguing, and that he continued to seem stressed over the next few days, part of me was glad. He's been so lonely. Things have been better lately with him forming such strong friendships with all of us, but...." She shrugged.

And finally, I caught on. At the notion, I had a sense of what I figured Athena was feeling. The thought of Paulie having a relationship was comforting. Though maybe awful to think, Paulie was the type of man who clearly struggled in that venue. Forming friendships had been hard enough for him. The idea of him having a romance was nearly inconceivable, which was maybe why it had taken me so long to clue in.

The door to the waiting room opened. Katie popped up from her chair as we all looked over.

There was a collective sigh of disappointment.

"Trust me, I'm not relishing spending time with any of you either." Officer Susan Green scowled in the doorway. She cast a glance at Athena. "No disrespect intended to you, of course."

Look at that, someone Susan Green actually liked.

"Sorry, Susan." Leo, ever more gracious than myself, remained pleasant. "We've been waiting for word on Paulie. We thought you were the doctor or nurse with an update."

"I asked when I came in. He's still in surgery. They hope to have more details within the hour." Her hard, pale blue eyes softened. "We're all pulling for him. It's a hard night for the Merchants. We've already lost one of our players; we're not going to lose another one."

Every time I was close to writing the woman off as nothing more than a cold-hearted tyrant, she went and surprised me. And she highlighted my own shortcomings. How much I was thinking of Paulie, and how little I was considering Melody, and maybe more importantly at this point, the pain and loss Jared was experiencing. His hysteria had been part of the reason I'd been released so quickly from the scene. By that point, the Estes Park police and I'd had so many encounters over dead bodies that, protocol or not, I wasn't considered a suspect. Branson told me to go be with Paulie, that he'd catch up with me later.

Maybe something had held Branson up. "Are you here for me?"

Susan's gaze didn't harden back to the place it had been when she entered, but it didn't stay soft or compassionate either. "I am. Come talk to me out here. I have a room for us."

Casting a glance at the other three and feeling like I was walking to the principal's office, I followed Susan down the hallway and into a small clinic room a few doors down.

"I have your bare-bones statement that you gave to Sergeant Wexler." She launched in the second the door was closed. "You say you went to the pet shop to pick up a hat for your dog." Her head cocked, and she glanced at my feet. "Where is he? I thought you two were attached by an umbilical cord or something."

"He's at home. I didn't figure the hospital would look fondly upon him being here." I focused on keeping my tone neutral, though I felt my temper bubbling. Susan was always great at igniting that particular pilot light. "And I didn't want to be excluded from seeing Paulie if the chance arose."

She straightened as she lifted her chin. "Sometimes you surprise me Winifred Page, actually displaying some common sense and courtesy."

Susan was my exact height, but where I was soft and curvy, she looked like she was ready to audition for the *American Gladiators* show. Her frequent physical posturing only served to heighten my irritation in her presence. "Can we skip this part, please? We're both aware that we're not exactly each other's favorite person in the world. But my friend is fighting for his life. I'm not in the mood."

"You have a point." To my surprise, though she wouldn't apologize for it, Susan seemed abashed. "Well, as I was saying, it says that you were there to pick up a special order, you found Melody Pitts dead behind the counter, and then discovered Paulie in the back room, which is when you called 911. Is that correct?"

I nodded. "It is."

"Are you certain Melody was already deceased when you found her? Did you check for vitals or disturb the scene?"

"No, I didn't check." I paused half a heartbeat to remind myself that at the end of the day, Susan was simply doing her job. "And no, I did not disturb the scene. I determined that she was dead just by looking at her."

"The same can't be said for Mr. Mertz, correct? You disturbed the scene there." Her tone made it sound more like a question than accusation.

"That's true. I started to make the call, but then Watson discovered Paulie. I rushed to my friend, not thinking, and only then noticed that he was alive.

That's when I dialed 911. That's also when Jared came in and discovered Melody."

Susan scratched some notes, and if I wasn't mistaken, used the time to get her emotions in check. It seemed she truly cared about her softball teammates. Maybe even Paulie. When she looked back at me, though, she was the woman she always was with me. "Any items of evidence that might have wandered into your purse or pockets? Maybe smuggled out with your little dog?"

"Of course not."

She simply shrugged. "I don't know why you think that's an unreasonable question. It's not like it would be the first time." Before I could retort, she flipped her notebook shut with a little snap. "Well, if you have nothing more helpful to offer, then I guess we're done here."

Despite not wanting to linger with Susan, I couldn't keep from asking, even though I knew the expression and tone I would receive. "I was under the impression that Branson was going to come by to take my statement. Is he okay?"

Sure enough disdain filled her gaze and sarcasm dripped from every syllable. "Sergeant Wexler has a job to do, Ms. Page. And as evidenced by your statement, you have nothing more helpful to provide, so he is better utilized elsewhere. As am I." She started to walk away, then turned back. "I'm to remind you that this is a police matter. We have it well under control, and that any snooping you and your little fleabag might do will only muddy the waters."

"You're to remind me of that?" I stepped back and took my turn lifting my chin in defiance. "You really expect me to believe that Branson sent you with that message?"

"Trust me, Ms. Page, I neither expect nor care if you believe me or not. I am simply the messenger." She lifted a finger. "Oh, on that note, there was one other thing I was supposed to pass on. Even though I am not a delivery service. Sergeant Wexler mentioned that you had inquired on what would happen with Paulie's dogs. Dr. Sallee picked them up. They will be housed at the Estes Park Animal Clinic." That time she made it across the room and looked back from the open door. "If you happen to think of any information that might *actually* be helpful, feel free to give me a call. Or... if you stumble into some evidence in your pockets, purse, or under your puppy's collar, be sure to pass it along."

I stared at the closed door for several seconds after she left. Though I was certain Branson hadn't used any of those terms that Susan had chosen, he was the only one I'd asked about what was going to happen with Flotsam and Jetsam. Clearly, he had sent that message with Susan Green. The realization stung. After another moment, I reminded myself not to jump to conclusions, and more importantly, whatever was happening between Branson and me didn't matter compared to Paulie's struggle in the operating room. When I was certain I had my irritation under control, I returned to the others.

The windows of my little log cabin displayed scenes that could've easily doubled as Colorado postcards. The summer evening was peaceful, calm, serene. The surrounding forest of pine and aspen trees were enchantingly hazy in the soft light of dusk. The mountains silhouetted behind them gave an air of mystery and romance, the last vestiges of snow at their peaks offered a hint of whimsy. I was willing to bet some mother rabbit was tucking her little babies into bed in a cozy little burrow, while a majestic owl stretched its wings as it woke, readying for its nightly activities. Paradise.

Most nights, the interior of my home mimicked the serenity of our surroundings. After dinner, I'd curl up in front of the fire, even if I had to leave the windows open to keep from getting too hot, and read while Watson napped at my feet.

That was true, for most nights.

"What are they doing?" Gary sat on the far side of the sofa, his ex-football-player build accentuated as he remained in a constant state of movement while he watched the unending chaos.

"The better question is what *aren't* they doing?" Percival's lips curved in distaste as he addressed me. "There's being a good friend, Fred, and then there's taking being a martyr beyond the Joan of Arc status."

I was beginning to agree with him. "They've been like this for hours." I bugged my eyes at my uncles. "*Hours.*" I motioned to Watson, who'd taken refuge in the corner of the room, wedging himself between the wall and a cabinet. "And that one hasn't stopped glaring at me since we got home."

"I can't say I blame him." Percival lifted his long, thin legs as Flotsam and Jetsam deviated from their repeated path—which began in my bedroom, went through the living room, into the kitchen, out the doggy door where they did Lord only knew what to the dog run, and then circled back—to take several frantic laps around the sofa before once more disappearing into the kitchen, followed by a loud clatter. "When your mother said she and Barry were busy assisting the girls at the shop and you were needing some help, I didn't think twice. I'm not used to my sister being deceptive, but I'm starting to wonder if Phyllis exaggerated the needs of setting up the shop so she wouldn't have a heart attack at the way these monsters are treating our childhood home."

"It will end soon. It has to." I raked my fingers nervously through my hair. "They have to fall asleep sometime, right?"

"Demons don't sleep, darling." Percival flinched from another loud crash in the kitchen. "Why don't you call Dr. Sallee? Tell him you changed your mind. That they can stay at the clinic after all."

That thought began circling my mind nearly as quickly as Flotsam and Jetsam entered my home. "I can't. Leo and Athena are taking care of the pet shop while Paulie's in the hospital. I have to do something."

Gary splayed out his hands in an *isn't it obvious* gesture. "You're going to solve his murder... er... attempted murder. I say that's more than enough. In fact, this distraction could make that harder. Shove them off on Katie. She can handle it."

"She's going to take as much time as she can off work and sit by Paulie's side at the hospital. They don't know how long it'll be before he wakes up, or... if he will, but one of us needs to be there at all times, just in case. And besides, who said I was solving anything?"

Percival gave an exaggerated eyeroll, but before he could offer commentary, Gary smiled indulgently. "Don't even bother playing that card, dear. We all know you probably have a hundred theories already as to what happened. You'll figure it out; my bet is before Paulie heals enough to wake up." His smile altered to one of compassion. "And he will, Fred. He's got to."

I knew all too well that life didn't quite work how we mortals thought it was supposed to, that there were no guarantees for Paulie. There hadn't been any for Melody, after all. Still, I couldn't quite bring myself to admit that not only did I not have a hundred theories, but that the only theory I did possess was little more than some mystery woman one of the town locals didn't even recognize.

Flotsam and Jetsam tore back through the living room, into the bedroom, where there was a skirmish of barks and then reemerged once more, Jetsam with Watson's chipmunk stuffed animal in his mouth, and Flotsam close at his heels. They nearly reached the kitchen when Jetsam stumbled on something, apparently air, and tumbled in a roll. Flotsam took advantage of the moment, snagged the chipmunk, and disappeared into the kitchen. The dog door flapped loudly as he disappeared into the dog run. Bounding up as if falling was the most fun he'd ever had, Jetsam frolicked away and disappeared outside as well.

In the corner, Watson growled.

I gave him a glare of my own. "Oh, stop it. That was your least favorite toy anyway."

"Forget the toy. Those two will destroy your dog run. The thing hasn't even been built a year, and you spent a fortune on it." Percival sounded aghast.

"And that fortune guaranteed it was indestructible. This will be the test." I sank back into the overstuffed armchair, bordering on exhaustion. Maybe they were right. Perhaps taking care of the two corgis was a bit too much. For Watson *and* myself. And they were right about the other thing too. Of course I was going to try to figure out who hurt Paulie and killed Melody, and not having a moment's peace to grab some sanity wouldn't help that process.

"We can come over and babysit here and there if you need a break, Fred." Gary's low, soft rumbling voice always reminded me of my father. Especially in times like these, where he was being so kind.

"What?" Percival sat ramrod straight and went

ultrasonic. "Are you trying to get a divorce? May I remind you that you forfeited a prenup!"

Gary gave a small eye roll and shook his head, not bothering to look at his husband. "We'll do whatever we can to help out, Fred."

"Thank you. That means the world." And it did. I also knew I would never ask that of them. Percival got along well enough with Watson, in the way that two aloof individuals tolerate each other, but he was not an animal person. My uncles had been together for decades. Even with their constant squabbles, I couldn't imagine anything pulling them apart, but if anything could be that powerful, it would be Flotsam and Jetsam, I had no doubt.

As if reading my mind, Percival took on a serious, yet know-it-all tone. "How about we just skip all this. I already know who did it. And I don't mind sharing. You can even claim full ownership of it, Fred. Tell everyone you solved it. Just get these dogs out of our lives."

Though Gary gave another combo of eye roll and headshake, I couldn't help but lean forward. "You know? How in the world would you know?"

"He doesn't." Gary glowered at Percival. "He and Anna Hanson got lost in a gossip fest for a couple of hours today."

Percival swatted at him before he could keep going. "Oh sure, say it like that, like you and Carl weren't just as much a part of it."

Gary swiveled to face him. "Maybe we were, but at least we know the difference between gossip and fact."

"That's okay, gossip or fact, doesn't matter. It's at least a place to start." I could feel where this was headed. In another thirty seconds this would go from bickering into a full-out argument. I held Percival's gaze. "Who is it? Who do you think?"

He nodded in satisfaction and sat a little straighter. "Well... I might've exaggerated, slightly." He cast a quick glare toward Gary, but refocused on me quickly enough. "I don't know *exactly* who, but I have it narrowed down to two possible suspects."

Gary groaned.

"Well, I *do*." Percival sniffed. "And, if Anna's theory is right, then it could qualify as one suspect."

"Okay, then what's her theory?" Anna and Carl owned Cabin and Hearth and were the reigning gossip champions of Estes Park, followed closely by my uncles. Though they typically required a grain of salt, or a truckload of it, they were often at least somewhat on the right track.

"Well, darling, I wouldn't exactly say it's Anna's theory per se. After all, I came up with the two suspects. She just happened to put them together."

Gary dropped his head into his hands, groaning once more.

I nearly laughed but was too desperate to have this over with to give in to the humor. "Fine, then who are your suspects?"

Percival paused, clearly for effect, took a deep breath, then answered in the form of an announcement. "Margie Miller and Jared Pitts, of course."

I shook my head instantly. "No. Not possible. I was there when Jared discovered Melody's body. His reaction was genuine. No way was he faking that."

"He's new in town, darling. We don't know what he's capable of." Percival was clearly offended one of his suspects was met with disapproval.

"Jared didn't have anything to do with it. I guarantee it." Even as I said it, I could hear my father's chastising voice—he'd always said during investigation you couldn't let your feelings or assumptions get in the way. But he'd also said you had to trust your gut. And my gut said Jared was devastated over Melody's murder. "And as for the other one, Margie, you said? Who is...?" Her last name was the only other clue I needed. "Pete Miller's wife? The glassblower? Why in the world would she...?" Again, my voice trailed off. I was speaking too fast, before my brain could catch up, but as it did, the memory of the softball game the day before rushed in. "Oh."

Percival nodded in satisfaction. "Honestly, Fred, I'm a little surprised you didn't arrive there yourself." He gestured toward the kitchen and the muffled noises sounding from the dog run. "You've been through a lot today, so it makes sense you wouldn't be at the top of your game. However, I heard about the drama between Pete and Jared. The whole town did."

Despite the fight on the field being broken up fairly quickly, I was certain Percival was right; that juicy tidbit would have spread through the town like wildfire. And I was willing to bet I hadn't been the only one to notice Melody and Pete and what looked like a whispered conversation before Delilah had interrupted them. "You think they were having an affair. Melody and Pete?"

"Obviously." Percival nodded.

As Gary spoke, he nearly sounded apologetic. "Clearly, we don't know Melody, but Pete has an eye for pretty things. Not just those made of glass. In fact, it's not only—"

The three of us jumped at the knock at the door. Proving their large ears weren't just for looks alone, Flotsam and Jetsam let out a torrent of howls and barks while crashing back into the living room and nearly coming unhinged as they reared up, pounding the door with their paws. Watson yipped and retreated farther into the corner.

I glanced at the clock on the mantle. "It's nearly nine. Who in the world could that be?"

I crossed the room, and Percival and Gary followed behind protectively. Probably more from being on edge from Paulie's corgis as opposed to truly being worried about a killer politely knocking.

"Hush, you two. You're fine." I attempted to pet Flotsam and Jetsam on their heads in what I hoped was a soothing manner, but it only increased their frantic hysteria. I literally had to push between and shove them aside with my legs to bring my eye to the peephole.

As the face came into view in the glow of the front porch light, my heart rate decided to match that of the insane corgi team.

Branson.

Maybe he really had simply been caught up and too busy to come question me at the hospital and was now here to explain, maybe apologize, for sending Susan in his place.

Attempting to shush the corgis again to no avail, I opened the door, which proved to not be such a simple task with the two of them still pounding against it.

Branson stepped in, his face scrunched up in pain at the shrill barking. His green eyes darted to me in confusion and then Percival and Gary before looking down at the dogs, then back up at me. "How long have they been like this, or is it just because I'm here?"

"Hours. Although slightly more intense after the knock on the door."

He scowled, then refocused on the dogs. "Shut up!" His bark of the command was even louder than the dogs, and caused Percival, Gary, and myself to flinch again.

Flotsam and Jetsam whimpered.

"I said shut up!" Branson stomped his foot.

The corgis stood there, trembling, and then darted off at the same moment, proving they shared one mind, and disappeared back into the dog run.

Typically, such a display of yelling at animals in such a tone would have brought out my fury. Instead, though it made me feel slightly guilty, a wave of relief washed over me. "Dear Lord, thank you."

"Are you watching them for Paulie?"

I nodded, feeling a fool.

He gave a slow shake of his head that clearly communicated he thought I was a glutton for punishment. "Well, if you happen to murder them before Paulie wakes up, I'll cover for you."

My uncles had stepped forward, and Percival patted Branson on the chest, his touch lingering just a second longer than it needed to. "Handsome and a slayer of dragons." He gave me a knowing look. "Snatch this one up, darling niece, or I'll trade in my Benedict Arnold over here for an upgrade." He glared at Gary before muttering, "Offering to take in those two demons. Really." He took me by the shoulders and kissed me quickly on the cheek. "We're going to get out of your hair now. The last thing you need are two old men killing the mood. Looks like those monsters are finally under control."

Gary followed him, giving me a quick kiss. "Wish me luck. Your uncle is going to be insufferable tonight." He waved over his shoulder at Watson before disappearing out into the night.

After shutting the door, I turned to Branson, expecting him to be grinning or offer some clever comments about my zany uncles. Instead his arms were folded, his expression serious. "What is it? Is Paulie okay? Did he take a turn for the worse?"

"No." He softened, just slightly. "Sorry. Far as I know, there's been no change. Still in critical condition, but as stable as he can be."

Another wave of relief washed over me. "Thank God." Remembering my manners and that things had been rather tense between us as we parted from our date, I gestured toward the sofa. "Come in, have a seat. Would you like some hot tea?" I debated for a moment, considered offering him glass of wine, but decided against it. I was too tired and too frazzled to think clearly about anything, let alone Branson. "Maybe some decaf coffee?"

"Thank you, but no. This isn't a social call." Branson unfolded his arms but remained standing at attention and didn't make a move toward the sofa.

Watson waddled over and plopped down, pressing against my leg.

I glanced at him, surprised. I expected nothing but irritated dismissiveness until the other corgis were gone, probably long after. Instead, Watson seemed like he was standing with me in solidarity against something. Like he knew something I didn't.

With my sense of dread growing, I turned back

to Branson. "Okay, then, if it's not a social call, what can I do for you?"

Branson hesitated, just for a moment, and in that heartbeat those green eyes softened again. I could see the debate in their depths, but then the wall slammed shut behind them and they turned as hard as bricks. "I know Susan talked to you earlier. I wanted to come by to reiterate. To let you know it's expected that you'll let the police handle this."

I gaped at him, waiting for more. None came.

No words came to me, either. At least quickly.

This was old stuff. From when I'd first moved to Estes. But Branson and I were past it, way past it. To the point that over the past several months, we'd almost felt like partners at times, in certain ways. "What's the catch?"

"There is no catch." Though his voice wasn't unfriendly, his tone communicated that there was no room for argument or discussion. "This is police business. You need to stay out of it. Be there for Paulie, sell books. You do what you do; we'll do what we do."

A flash of hurt tore through me, almost shocking how deep it cut. Thankfully, it was swiftly stampeded by red-hot anger. "I'm pretty certain we've covered this before, quite a while ago in fact. I don't appreciate being told what to do."

"I'm sorry about that, but it can't be helped. This is police business. It has nothing to do with you, so again, I repeat, stay out of it." Once more his voice was emotionless, cold and professional. If there'd been sarcasm or even condescension, it might've hurt less, though probably made me no less furious.

"And what brought this on? One minute you're admiring my skills at solving murders, which I feel inclined to point out I've done a lot quicker than those of you who call it your business."

He winced, but either wasn't going to say anything or I continued too quickly.

"So why now? Why is this case untouchable?"

"And there you go, acting like you're entitled to information from the police. You're not, Fred." His eyes hardened possibly further. "You're a bookseller. Your *dad* was the detective, not you. Focus on selling books."

Maybe I only saw what I wanted to, but I would've sworn he was making himself say these things. Intentionally being cruel for some purpose. Like a mother bird shoving her young from the nest so they could fly. Or spanking a child who ran out into the street so they'd learn their lesson and not get hurt in the future.

Well... I was neither a bird nor a child. "I have

never broken the law or gotten in the way of the police. I won't this time either."

"*This* time?" He took a step forward, paused when I straightened, then moved back again. "Didn't I just make myself clear? You're to stay out of the way on this one. If you don't, there will be consequences."

Watson growled, making it clear I wasn't imagining the tone in Branson's voice.

"Consequences?" Hurt trumped the fury in that moment. "I remember a time you told my dog that you would never hurt his mother. Ever."

"Fred...." For the first time, his shoulders slumped. "I will *never* hurt you. I meant legal consequences, clearly."

I wasn't so sure. "You need to get out of my house. Now."

There was no doubt that what flashed in front of those brick walls in his eyes was hurt. So much that I nearly second-guessed myself. But then it was gone. He straightened once more. "Of course." He reached out, but paused with his grip on the door handle. "I swear, Winifred Page, you will *always* be safe with me. But this isn't personal; you are to stay out of this. If you step a foot out of line, I won't hesitate to do my job."

"Step a foot out of line. Why you...." I realized I was shaking. That and my hands were balled into fists, my nails digging into the meat of my palms.

Watson continued to growl, and over Branson's shoulders, I saw Flotsam and Jetsam standing in the doorway of the kitchen both on full alert, almost like they were awaiting Watson's orders.

I looked Branson dead in the eyes and made my voice as hard as I could, though it required no effort in that moment. "I thought I told you to get out."

Without another word, he nodded and walked out the door.

I slammed the door behind him and twisted the deadbolt.

At my feet, Watson whined as I sank to the floor, resting my back against the door, and took his handsome face into my hands. "Everything's okay, my brave boy. Good boy. Good boy."

He answered with a lick to my cheek.

After a moment I held my hand out toward Flotsam and Jetsam. "You guys too. Good job. Get over here."

Though they rushed, stumbling, neither barked as they approached, and at Watson's warning growl, they slowed.

I don't know how long I sat there, petting them,

taking comfort in all three dogs. Even so, the length of time, whatever it was, didn't even begin to quench my fury.

I was going to figure out who hurt Paulie and killed Melody in record time. That, or die trying.

"Don't do it. Don't you move." I raised my finger in the air as well as my voice, taking on the tone I'd used when I was a professor.

To my surprise, both Flotsam and Jetsam promptly sat obediently on the kitchen floor, looking unusually cute with the mint-green appliances behind them. I supposed they were probably cute all the time, when their insanity wasn't so distracting.

"Good job." I tried to keep the surprise out of my tone, afraid that if a crack showed in my confidence, they'd run amok. "Now for the real test. Both of you stay right there while Watson has his breakfast."

Though he'd done just fine asserting his dominance in his own right the night before, I wanted to reinforce it. It was Watson's home, after all. And as much as I wanted to take care of Paulie's babies, I wasn't going to do so if the cost was having Watson trembling in a corner for the duration of their stay. I remembered how some animal documentary about lions or wolves or something had said the ruler of the pack always ate first.

As I set Watson's food in front of him, I prepared for both of us to be run over by the frantic twosome.

Apparently deciding to not take any chances, Watson devoured his food in record time.

Though they whimpered pitifully, Flotsam and Jetsam showed remarkable restraint as Watson speed-ate. Judging from their dramatic trembling, the force of will came at a cost.

Once finished, Watson cast a superior glance at them and then sauntered into the living room.

"Good job, boys. Your turn."

As I set the two bowls of baked chicken in front of them, they became unhinged, their true natures revealed. Snorting and snuffling, they pushed and shoved each other as they scarfed down their breakfast. Fearing I might lose a hand, I moved out of the way. Even though they both ate out of each other's bowls and flecks of food spread over my floor, it seemed they managed to get an equal amount.

I leaned against the counter, crossed my arms, and gave a determined nod as the two corgis moved on to cleaning up the mess they'd made over the hardwood. I'd barely gotten any sleep the night before in my fury at Branson, but between the fire of that flame and the copious amounts of caffeine I'd already had that morning, I didn't feel the least bit tired. If anything, the lack of sleep only served to strengthen my determination. And if Flotsam and Jetsam were any indicator, I was off to a good start.

I wasn't going to allow myself to be ruled by corgis named after a Disney supervillain's sidekicks, and that was doubly true for Branson Wexler.

Every so often, a part of my brain tried to figure out the *why* of it all. I was certain he had his reasons. The core of the man was kind, and despite the tense interaction of the night before, I did believe I was safe with him. There had to be something going on that would cause him to act that way.

I only gave credence to those thoughts for a few moments. It didn't matter if I was safe with him, if he was good at heart, nor if he turned loose a fluttering flock of butterflies in my stomach when we were near.

I'd promised myself I would never be told what to do again, and most definitely not in the manner in which he'd attempted to do so in my own home. Not only was I going to ignore every word the man said, but I was going to figure out who was responsible for Paulie and Melody, and do so in record time.

In that vein, I'd already texted Katie and Ben to let them know I would be majorly late arriving to the Cozy Corgi. There'd been many times in the past where I'd left Katie to manage both the bakery and the bookstore on her own, or simply hadn't opened it at all while I... interfered with police business, as Branson had said. Ben was a godsend in more than one way. Plus, with Nick working with Katie, there were three people managing the place. I could walk away and not give it a second thought. Which was perfect.

Leaving Flotsam and Jetsam to have the run of the house and dog run, Watson and I popped into my volcanic-orange Mini Cooper and headed to town. I knew exactly where to start.

I'd only been into Hot Air a handful of times, but I couldn't imagine ever entering the glassblowing store and not being captivated by the beauty. In a similar fashion to my bookshop, though this one was free-standing, the shop was laid out like a little house, winding around and offering various themes of hand-blown glass in different rooms. With the exception of the rear of the house, all the walls were solid windows, making the place feel as if it were part of the outside. The space was bright, airy, clean, and absolutely filled to overflowing with colorful glass. Platters, bowls, vases, and assorted dishes glistened on shelves and over tabletops, in colors ranging from candy-cane-like stripes to speckles to a swirling, elevated take on tie-dyed patterns. Large other-worldly garden balls attached to iron spikes looked like clusters of giant lollipops protruding out of aluminum buckets. Overhead, strung like criss-crossing lights, hung glass balls and Christmas orna-ments. Cabinets displayed intricate glass figures, ranging from mythical unicorns and mermaids to every example of wildlife Estes Park had to offer.

Perhaps if Pete Miller wasn't the one who'd murdered Melody and nearly killed Paulie, I'd see if he could create a little corgi for me. I was definitely getting ahead of myself with that thought.

Watson stayed close to my side. Despite it being well before noon, the place was packed with tourists, to the point I wondered how often people ran into things and sent glass shattering everywhere. Not that I'd really considered it, but I was doubly thankful I'd left Flotsam and Jetsam at the house. I wasn't certain what destruction I might come home to, but the idea of them in a glassblowing studio was worse than anything a bull could do to a china shop.

In the corner of the largest room, behind a wall of what appeared to be chicken wire, was the workspace itself. Benches lined the front so people could sit and watch as Pete Miller and a young girl, who I assumed was his apprentice or employee, created more glass artworks.

I joined the crowd, standing behind a cluster of kids crowding one of the benches. To avoid the countless feet, Watson took shelter under my skirt.

Despite my determination to hit the ground running, I found myself captivated. The times I'd been in before, the workspace had been empty. Watching Pete and his assistant work was like observing wizards performing magic.

Pete stood over what I figured was a sort of kiln—a long, cylindrical metal tube with a small hole in the front—and spun a long metal rod between his hands. A fiery orange blob glowed on the end within the blazing inferno inside the tube. Even from twenty feet away, the heat washed over us. From a distance, it was pleasant, almost cozy, but I couldn't imagine what it felt like from Pete's perspective.

On the other side of the space, the apprentice held thin sticks of glass to a small flame. She spoke softly to the people directly in front of her, explaining the process as her hands never stopped moving. Narrowing my eyes, I realized she was creating a hummingbird. She must be responsible for all the glass figurines in the cabinets.

My attention was drawn back to Pete as he pulled the glowing orb from the fire, closed the door to cut off the wave of heat rolling over us, and blew into the end of the tube as he continued to spin it between his hands.

It truly was magic. The orb expanded like a balloon, growing so large I thought it would burst. Then, never ceasing in his spinning motion, he brought it to the countertop just on the other side of the chicken wire directly in front of the observers, then rolled it over shards of colored glass.

Then he blew again, and this time the orb had streaks of color in it.

Pete repeated the process a couple of different times, and though I couldn't figure out how it happened, even as I watched, the orb became a vase, and as it cooled, the glowing orange transitioned to deep cobalt blue with flecks of silver and violet. It was lovely, and the entire process took my breath away.

As Pete continued his craft, forming a pedestal

for the vase, I studied him. Maybe my uncles had been wrong, maybe what I'd noticed on the softball field had been nothing more than me jumping to conclusions. Surely a man who could create such fragile and sublime beauty wouldn't be cheating on his wife. Surely such an artist who devoted his life to creation wouldn't kill someone.

And maybe... if I wasn't my father's daughter, if I hadn't seen so much of life, I could have pretended that such notions might be how the world worked. But I knew better.

As Pete put the finishing touches on the vase, his gaze traveled over his audience. He looked past me and then returned, his eyes locking with mine in recognition. There was a flash of something, maybe fear, maybe irritation, I couldn't tell, but then he moved on.

Clearly, he knew I wasn't there because I was looking for decorations for my home.

In the few minutes it took him to finish the vase, his demeanor altered from one of ease and an almost Zen-like trance as he worked to stiff robotic movements. After placing the vase in another oven contraption, he went to the girl who was still working on the hummingbird, whispered something, and then kissed her temple before exiting the workspace. He caught my gaze once more and made a motion with his head for me to follow him.

That, I hadn't been expecting.

It only took me a moment to follow, managing to step over Watson without getting my foot caught in my skirt or in his leash, and the two of us walked around the tourists, following to where Pete disappeared into the back. I spared a glance at the apprentice. She was clearly much too young to be his wife, unless Pete had truly robbed the cradle. Yet he'd kissed her for everyone to see.

Maybe he and his wife had an arrangement. I'd heard of such things.

Pete stood at the back door, which opened to the outside. If it had led to some dark storeroom or something, I wouldn't have followed, but we walked out to a charming flower garden that overlooked the parking lot at the base of the mountain and a few of the other stores. There was a small wrought-iron set of table and chairs that had been painted white, surrounded by some of those glass garden balls sticking out of flowering bushes in whimsical clusters.

Again, the idea of the man who created spaces like this being the one responsible for Melody and Paulie seemed ludicrous. Not to mention that I didn't have even the slightest tingle of apprehension at following him.

Pete motioned toward one of the iron chairs. "Have a seat. I figure I know why you're here." His tone wasn't overly friendly, but neither did it sound aggressive.

"Okay, thank you." I did as he asked, and Watson settled in below the chair, as if preparing for a nap. It seemed he wasn't experiencing any apprehension either. Since Pete was being direct, I decided to follow his lead. "Are you okay with me being here?" There were a few storeowners in town who took great offense when I decided to look into things they determined were none of my business.

Pete shrugged as he sat across from me. "I suppose. You have a reputation around town, and while I don't really understand why you're involved, if it helps figure out what happened to Melody, then I'll talk to just about anybody."

Direct indeed. I hadn't expected that either. "I take it you were close to Melody Pitts?"

"Very. She was a wonderful woman." Though his eyes remained dry, his voice sounded tight, pained.

It seemed my uncles weren't wrong after all. The

man was clearly grieving. "We only met her once, but she seemed very kind."

"She was." Pete took a steadying breath and then met my gaze once more. "So, why are you here to see me? How can I help?"

If he was responsible, Pete Miller was the best actor in the world. So much so, that I almost considered cutting him off my suspect list. But then again, he hadn't really been on that list to begin with. That was his wife. But, determined though I was to settle this quickly, I also didn't want to cause damage to a marriage, and I needed to get a good read on the man before I spoke to his wife. After what I'd observed with his assistant, that almost took Margie off my suspect list as well. If he was so obvious with his affection toward other women, there had to be aspects to their marriage I didn't understand. "You can help by telling me about your affair."

"What?" His flinch was so exaggerated and so violent that it startled me, and Watson emerged from underneath my chair on full alert. "Tell you about my what?"

I had to take a second to recalibrate after his reaction. It seemed he wasn't going to be as forthright as I'd supposed. "Your affair. I'd like you to tell me about your affair."

"I... affair...." His cheeks went a vibrant shade of crimson over the scruff of his jaw, and he looked around in a panic. "I don't know what you mean."

It was almost laughable. His guilt couldn't be more evident than if he had a scarlet *A* sewn onto his chest. "Maybe you and your wife call it something else. Clearly the two of you have an agreement of some sort. Some kind of arrangement."

Genuine confusion crossed his features, lessening some of the panic. "What in the world are you talking about?"

Feeling like I was a little crazy, I motioned back toward the studio. "Well... like right in there. Kissing your assistant in front of everyone. That's hardly keeping things secret."

He flinched again before his confusion gave way to disgust. "That's Abby, my *daughter*."

It was my turn to flinch. *His daughter.*

Good Lord, talk about playing the part of the fool. That's what I got for listening to gossip without doing a little more investigating first. Pete had just seemed so transparent when we'd sat down I'd.... I paused in that train of thought, remembering his initial reaction to the mention of the affair. I hadn't been imagining that. I was certain.

"Okay, sorry about that. I didn't realize she was

your daughter. But that doesn't change the facts." I decided to double down. If nothing else, clearly the man had absolutely no poker face; whatever reaction he had would tell me something. "It's hardly a secret around town that you're having an affair."

Again the panic rose to his face, and his gaze actually darted around as if he expected pitchfork-wielding villagers to be surrounding him, or maybe just his wife.

I pushed harder. "I even noticed it myself during the softball game on the Fourth of July. Anybody with eyes could have seen it. Right there, out in the open. Your affair was clear as day to everyone." Close enough to the truth.

With a lurching motion, his elbows banging against the tabletop, he leaned forward, his voice a frantic whisper. "Be quiet. Don't say that so loud."

From his reaction, there was no doubt about the affair, none.

He confirmed it before I even had a chance to push again. "Have you talked to my wife? Have you talked to Margie? Please don't. Please. She doesn't know. She doesn't need to. I don't want to hurt her."

Though I couldn't understand how both those statements were true—the admission of an affair and genuine concern about hurting his wife—clearly he meant them. "So, you admit that you're having an affair, Pete?"

"Yes. Fine, yes." For the first time, tears shimmered in his eyes, guilt clearly evident. "I am. But I've been trying to stop, been trying to quit. I will. I promise I will. Just don't say anything to Margie."

I nearly did a double take. "Trying to quit? I'd say that was handled for you, wouldn't you?"

Pete's mouth fell open, and he blinked. "What?"

It felt like we were going in circles. Perhaps that was exactly how he wanted it. "Well, Melody's dead. I'd say your affair is over."

He blinked again, rapidly, and then his gaze cleared with understanding. "You think Melody and I were having an affair? You said you noticed at the softball game that...."

As his words trailed off, my own understanding clicked into place. "Delilah. You're having an affair with Delilah, not Melody."

He reached over and grabbed my hand. "Whisper, please."

I hadn't been speaking much above a whisper, but probably hearing his secrets in the light of day seemed like screaming no matter what my volume. Delilah. That made sense from what I'd seen on the softball field, at least partly. Delilah had looked irritated when she'd interrupted Pete and Melody's conversation. Thinking back, that could easily have been jealousy. "You weren't having an affair with Melody, too?"

"God, no." He shook his head frantically. "Never. Jared and Melody are... were... becoming really good friends with Margie and me. They're our go-to double-date couple."

Something wasn't adding up. The rumors about him and Melody, the intense familiarity between the two of them I'd witnessed for myself. "Pete, I saw the way you and Melody were speaking; that wasn't just friendship."

"Yes, it was." He sighed before glancing around once more. "Melody knew about the affair between me and Delilah. She found out a couple of days before she... died. She was trying to help me break it off with Delilah. She'd given me an ultimatum. Either end it or she was going to tell Margie."

The man might be a brilliant artist, but I wondered about his mental capacity. Surely he realized what he was saying. "Melody gave you an ultimatum? She was going to tell your wife about your affair?"

He nodded. "Exactly."

Maybe he was more aware than I realized.

Perhaps he was laying it all on the table, so much so, that it intentionally would seem ridiculous to suspect him if he was implicating himself. "Did that make you angry at her? That she was nosing into your relationship?"

"Kinda, but Melody was a sweetheart. She just wanted...." He sucked in a breath as his eyes grew wide. "I didn't kill her because of that. I didn't kill her at all. I don't want Margie to find out, but I wouldn't kill to stop that happening."

Another detail from that afternoon came back to me. "What about Jared? You two got into a fight. Did he find out about you and Melody?"

For the first time, irritation truly cut through his voice. "I was *not* having an affair with Melody."

"Then why the fight?"

The guilt was back, washing away everything else. "Melody hadn't told him about Delilah and me. But he... figured it out right then. Or Delilah told him during the game." He shrugged and stared down at the ground. "She plays games like that. I don't know. But however he found out, he did. He's furious at me, or at least was.... I'm sure he's not even thinking about me right now. He couldn't understand why I would betray Margie that way." He looked close to tears. "I don't understand either.

Why I keep... with...." He shook his head as his words trailed away.

I believed him. At least, I thought I did. Either the man was a complete and utter mess, or he wanted me to think he was. I still had the sense he wasn't that good an actor. But if I was wrong, maybe even that was part of the act. It was clear he was desperate to keep the affair from his wife. If Melody was threatening to tell her, then Pete had more than ample motive.

And yet....

"You're on the softball team and in the Feathered Friends Brigade with Paulie. Did he know about your affair?"

That time his eyes flashed. "No wonder people say the things they do about you."

I sat a little straighter, stung.

He leaned forward once more, anger filtering through his voice. "Paulie is my friend... kinda. He might be annoying and weird, but I've learned to care about the little guy. I wouldn't hurt him. And no, Paulie didn't know about the affair. Unlike you, he minds his own business."

Pete stood. "If I hear that you said one word about Delilah and me to anybody, to *anybody*, I promise you, you'll regret it."

I couldn't stop myself, not that I needed to. "You really think you're going to convince me that you didn't hurt Melody or Paulie by threatening me?"

Once more he flinched as if the thought was nearly out of the realm of possibilities. "Good grief. What's wrong with you? I wasn't threatening your life. But I will call the police and get you for harassment, or sue you for slander, something. Keep your nose out of it. Leave me and my family alone." He headed back into the shop but paused at the doorway. "And get off my property."

Watson and I entered Madame Delilah's Old Tyme Photography and came to a screeching halt. Actually, *I* came to a screeching halt; Watson trotted a few more steps before coming to his own sudden stop when he reached the end of his leash with a jerk and glared back at me in accusation.

The store was a long narrow space, and at the very back, in full view, was a naked man sitting in a round aluminum trough.

I started to make a hasty retreat when the full picture came into view. Flanking him on either side were two women, one a brunette cowgirl wearing chaps and a cowhide vest—with nothing beneath the vest—and brandishing a pistol in either hand. On the other, a blonde clad in a skimpy Native American buckskin shift raised a tomahawk over the naked man's head.

Though ridiculous and most definitely racially insensitive—or downright offensive—I realized the man was supposed to be caught in midbath by the two women.

"Perfect, now, let's try one where the Indian maiden joins you in the bathtub. Cowgirl, you're not going to be happy about it, so grab that rope on the wall and wrap it around your man's neck." In front of the scene, a curvy redheaded saloon girl held an old-fashioned-looking camera and turned toward me. "Give me one second. I'm a little short-staffed today. Let me finish up with these clients, and I'll be with you. Make yourself at...." Her deep blue eyes widened in recognition, and she cocked her head. "Oh... interesting...." Her gaze flicked to Watson, then back to me. "I'm betting I don't have to tell you not to go anywhere. I'll be right with you, my little bookworm. Find an outfit you like while you wait." And with that, she turned back to the threesome who'd arranged themselves according to her specifications.

I glanced around the shop. I'd only been in once before, and Delilah hadn't been present. The place was done to look like a saloon in the old West. Wooden planks covered the walls, and tin photos—both black-and-white and sepia-toned varieties—

wallpapered nearly every available space and high-lighted all of the Western fantasy options available. From the looks of it, the naked person in the tub was a favorite. Though most of them weren't quite as risqué as the one unfolding in front of my eyes.

I'd come directly to Delilah's from the glassblowing studio after a brief debate with Watson as we walked down Elkhorn Avenue about whether we should go to Delilah's or find out where Margie Miller worked. Watson hadn't seemed to have a strong opinion either way, so I opted for Delilah's. I'd talk to Margie if I had to, but felt like I needed a specific plan if I was to speak to her. It wasn't clear how to get any information without sharing about her husband's affair. And though I thought she had the right to know, I didn't really feel like breaking up any marriages. Plus, it wasn't like Pete was going to warn Margie not to talk to me as he'd have to give a good reason as well. That wasn't true for Delilah. It was actually a relief to catch her with customers. It probably meant she hadn't heard from him yet.

I believed Pete. I truly didn't think he'd been having an affair with Melody. The man seemed about as transparent as the walls of his shop. But I wasn't completely convinced it hadn't been an act. If he truly was that obvious, I couldn't imagine how in the world he'd managed to keep his affair a secret from his wife. And while I doubted I could get Delilah to admit the affair outright, I figured she'd have some reaction when I asked that would give her away. At least enough to confirm if he'd been honest about that aspect.

In less than five minutes, the photoshoot was complete, and I was relieved to see when the man stood, he was wearing a pair of boxers that had been hidden behind the edge of the makeshift tub. Within another five minutes, they'd ordered a few eight-by-tens of multiple poses and Delilah told them to come back in two hours to pick them up. She followed the tourists to the door, locked it, and put up the Closed sign before turning to me.

"Winifred Page, we finally meet. I've heard about you, of course, and seen you from afar. I've been curious about the new redhead in town." The colorful layers of her taffeta saloon skirt, which was cut high in front and dragged the floor in back, rustled as she moved. And move she did, her body swaying like a snake. A seductive snake—though up until that moment, I hadn't realized such a concept existed. But it was apt. The woman dripped sensuality and felt dangerous.

"You don't need to close the shop just for me." Despite myself, I took a step backward.

"I figured you didn't want to be interrupted." Clearly having no sense of personal space, or more likely, enjoying invading it, Delilah stopped less than a foot and a half from me. She wasn't a small woman, and in her heels, she was a few inches taller than me. Nor was she dainty. But where I was curvy and soft, in a woman-next-door manner, Delilah was Marilyn Monroe, Jayne Mansfield, and Christina Hendricks all rolled into one. She lived up to her name from afar, but up close... though I hated to admit it, she brought out every physical insecurity I had. And from the pleased, venomous look in her eyes, she knew it. "I've heard plenty about you, and I know if you're here, that's because you suspect little old me of something sinister." Those full lips twitched. "Or to invite me to a book club, but I'm guessing the first option is the golden ticket." It seemed she liked the idea.

Before I could respond, as I was afraid I would stammer in an attempt to make actual words, Delilah knelt in a flurry of fabric and reached to Watson.

"And I've heard about you too." Her tone altered, and she sounded genuinely friendly. "You're just the cutest little tub of fluff I've ever seen."

To my astonishment, Watson didn't try to evade her affection. Didn't growl, back away, cringe, or do anything close to biting her hand off. He just sat there, tongue out, as he smiled and allowed himself to be adored.

For the first time in our relationship, I was tempted to step on his nub of a tail. It seemed Delilah charmed the males of every species. I couldn't help but feel somewhat betrayed.

Still petting Watson, Delilah peered up at me, her red waves of hair falling over her shoulders and down her back. "Did you pick out a look? I'll choose your cute little dog's outfit to complement yours. What's his name?"

"Watson." I was surprised how clear I could speak through gritted teeth. "But we're not here to get our picture taken."

"Yes, you are. If you want me to answer any questions." She simply smiled, gave a final pat to Watson's head, and stood. "And I'm assuming you're here because of that weird little Paulie being in the hospital and Ms. Goody Two-Shoes Melody getting herself killed. And trust me, I've got answers."

It had been a long, long time since I'd disliked anyone so much after such a short interaction. She made what I felt for Susan Green look like the two of us were bosom buddies, and the feeling was only heightened by Watson's clear acceptance of her. I bristled at how she spoke about Paulie, especially, and was tempted to tell her where she could stuff it and storm out of the shop. However, if it would help him, and help me to find out who had hurt Melody, I'd put up with the nasty woman for as long as I needed to. Swallowing my pride, I looked at the wall of costumes. "Fine. Whatever you want, just get it over with."

She cocked her head again, and her smile shifted. "Attitude. Huh. And here I thought I wouldn't like you." She narrowed her eyes, studying me and then grinned. "I know just the thing."

As she headed to the wall of costumes, it took all my willpower to keep from telling her to pick something that wasn't revealing. But I wasn't going to show any more weakness in front of her than I already had. If she suggested I strip down and get into the tub, that was exactly what I would do, and just pray no one I knew would walk by the large picture window that made up the front wall.

It only took her a matter of moments before she was back, thrusting a deep green dress into my hands. "You own a bookshop, and you look... smart. I'm thinking you're more retro than old West. Put this on." She pointed to a screen I'd not noticed in the far corner. "You can change there; you seem the modest type."

Temper flaring at the way she'd labeled me smart, her tone clearly indicating that the qualifier was akin to being as hideous as a goat beaten with the ugly stick, I took the dress and went behind the screen. Once there, I looked down, expecting to find Watson at my feet. He wasn't; the little traitor had stayed with Delilah.

I was going to give him salad for a week, while I ate cake in front of him.

To my surprise, Delilah had managed to select an outfit that fit me perfectly, and when I stepped in front of the mirror, it took effort not to suck in a breath of shock. I looked... beautiful, and she was right; it was exactly a style I would've chosen. The slinky flapper dress was bare at the arms and cut off at midthigh, striking a perfect balance of alluring and modest. Three layers of white fringe covered the lower portion and fell past my knees.

"Here. Let me put these on." Delilah stepped behind me and draped a necklace that was made of ropes and ropes of pearls around my neck. The final touch was a thin glittering band of white rhinestones around my head. Her reflection gave a nod over my shoulder. "There. You don't clean up too shabbily, do you?"

Only then did I notice Watson's reflection at my feet, and despite another wave of betrayal that he'd let someone put an outfit on him without bloodshed, I was utterly overcome with how adorable he was. He had a short Gatsby-styled tie around his neck and a small white fedora on his head, covering one of his ears.

Maybe I'd misjudged the woman. She hadn't taken the opportunity to humiliate me like I'd expected. And clearly, Watson approved of her.

"Now, go stand in front of the screen." She pointed to where the other three had been before, but now the background was an image of a gilded staircase beside a massive crystal chandelier. "I forgot to mention you're buying three copies of these, eight-by-tens, by the way. And unfortunately, since you haven't lived in town a year yet, I can't give you the local discount."

Strike that, I hadn't misjudged her after all.

Biting my tongue, I moved to where she'd suggested and patted my thigh so Watson would come over. If he didn't respond or chose to go stand by Delilah as she got her camera, I was going to threaten him with adopting Flotsam and Jetsam on a full-time basis. Thankfully for both of us, he complied and plopped down at my feet.

Delilah nodded her approval. "Perfect. Absolutely perfect. Now go ahead, little Nancy Drew, ask your questions while I adjust the settings. I have to admit I'm unbelievably curious how I got on your suspect list. I can't stand either of them, but there's only a couple of people in this world that I hate enough to murder, and neither Melody nor Paulie are important enough to make that list."

And I'd thought Pete had been transparent. Deciding to operate out of the same playbook as I had with him, I dove right in. "Are you having an affair with Pete Miller?"

"Really?" She looked up at me with a flash, pausing whatever she was doing to her camera. "*That's* what you want to ask? I must say I'm disappointed. From the rumors, I expected more from you."

I wasn't sure how to take that. I'd been insulted, but I wasn't exactly sure why. "You're not denying it."

She rolled her eyes. "Well, of course I'm not denying it. Every moron in town knows that I'm having an affair with Pete. Even his bore of a wife knows, though he's convinced she doesn't."

I blinked, completely thrown off by her easy admission of such a thing.

Delilah's second eye roll was even more dramatic. "Oh goodness, Winifred, you're supposedly a worldly, well-read woman; don't act so shocked. It's a tale as old as time. Men cheat on their wives. The wives just pretend not to notice. But even the ones who are too stupid to realize it would have to be brain-dead to not know about Pete and me. And as boring as Margie is, she isn't stupid." She held up the camera, snapped it, and continued talking. "The three of us went to high school together. We messed around behind her homely little back even then. I'm not entirely sure if Margie knew at the time, but I suspect she did."

After that, when I couldn't find my words, it was simply because I couldn't believe how truly reprehensible the woman was. And though I knew it wouldn't help, I couldn't keep my judgment to myself. "How can you talk about an affair in such a callous way? You're helping a man betray his marriage vows."

"Goodness, and here I hoped you wouldn't be so predictably puritanical, even with your Bible Belt roots." She lowered the camera to her jutted hip. "Any woman who thinks her husband isn't cheating is a fool. And I don't suffer fools. Or at least don't take away my own enjoyment of life because of their stupidity."

I gaped at her, earning yet another eye roll.

"Quit looking so surprised. Don't tell me you've never been cheated on."

I felt my cheeks burn.

"I thought so. You look like a divorcee." She nodded in satisfaction. "So, see, you know firsthand. You can attest. Somewhere in there, even if you didn't want to admit it to yourself, you knew that your husband was cheating. Probably almost from the very beginning."

I couldn't keep myself from flinching.

She'd started to raise the camera once more, but then her tone took on a pitiable quality. "Well, look at that. You really didn't know, did you?"

I didn't answer. The pain of my ex-husband's betrayal was long gone, but though I knew better, there were still times I felt I'd been played for a gullible fool. Clearly, Delilah agreed.

"That must've been awful for you. I'm sorry about that." She actually sounded like she meant it. "But that's how life is. Now you know, you won't be shocked again. And trust me, none of the men I sleep with are married to women so naïve. And even if

Margie had been originally, she isn't now. Not about me or the... *other* people Pete messes around with."

I couldn't take anymore. "I think we're done here." Without waiting, I stepped away from the photography set and headed toward the screen. I'd come for confirmation of Pete's affair, and I had more than gotten that, to say the least.

"That's totally fine. I've already got a couple of good shots here for you to choose from."

I nearly called out over the screen that she could dream on about me giving her a dime. But she felt like the type who would do everything in her power to get back at a perceived injustice. I could only imagine what she would say about the bookshop to the tourists who came into her store.

Delilah didn't wait for a response. "I have to ask, how in the world does me having an affair with Pete make me a suspect in your mind? You must have more imagination than you're demonstrating here if that's the case."

Though I bristled, I managed to keep my tone neutral as I struggled out of the flapper dress; it had been much easier to put on. "You're not on that list. Why, *should* you be?"

She gave a pleased giggle. "As fun as that would

be, no. But...." She paused, clearly letting the word linger, hoping I would give a reaction.

I didn't. Finally out of the dress, I started slipping into my real clothing.

"Oh, poo, you're absolutely no fun, book lady. But I'll tell you what, because I'm enamored of your little Watson here, I'll tell you for free."

Again she paused, but I didn't respond. In another few moments, I was dressed and stepped from behind the screen. Watson was out of costume as well and sat between us, smiling.

"There you are, back to your... pleasant self." She grinned her wicked smile, and I realize she'd been waiting so she could see my face. "I will tell you for free, but you have to pick. Do you want me to tell you the *who* or the *why*?"

"Are you insinuating you know who killed Melody and hurt Paulie?" I didn't think I'd ever met such a despicable person in my life. "You think this is a game, some fun little power play where you get to hold secrets?" I nearly trembled in rage.

That sensation only increased at Delilah's calm dismissal. "Please, take a breath. It's not *that* serious. I do know. Well... I don't know who *exactly*, but I have my suspicions, and I'm willing to bet I have more of them than you do, otherwise you wouldn't be here."

How I regretted I'd never taught Watson to attack on command.

Delilah moved behind the counter and patted the cash register. "Come, keep your end of the bargain, dear. And tell me, do you want the *who*, or the *why*?"

Feeling utter and complete self-loathing as I stepped up to the counter, which I figured was Delilah's point, I pulled out my credit card and managed to speak through gritted teeth one more time, though less clearly. "Who."

"It's your lucky day, not only do you get three eight-by-tens, but three shiny new suspects. They won't be as spectacular as me, but they'll actually want Melody and Paulie dead." She plucked the card from my hands and gave it a swipe. "Petra, Jared, and an unfortunate-looking blonde woman who's been sneaking around the back of Paulie's store." She winked. "See? I'm not the only one who enjoys an affair."

I gaped at her. "Jared didn't do it. No way. I saw his reaction. He was absolutely devastated. Further, why would Petra kill Melody and try to kill Paulie?

That makes no sense. And who's the woman you're talking about behind Paulie's store?"

"Now, now." She handed my card back and shook her finger. "You chose the who, remember? And if I knew who the woman was, I'd tell you. That was the deal."

I stuffed the card into my billfold and then jammed the thing into my purse. "This is *not* a game. What is wrong with you?"

"You know what? I'll throw in another couple freebies, just because I like you. Though I'm not really sure why. You're dreadfully tedious." She leaned forward, clearly showing off her perfect bosom in the low-cut saloon-girl dress. "Petra has plenty of reasons to hate Melody, but to be fair, lots of people did, not just Petra. Melody was completely insufferable. As far as Jared—well, refer to my last comment. And as for Paulie..., I don't know exactly what, but I can tell he doesn't simply look like a rat. He is one. That man has dirty little secrets practically gushing from his pores." Delilah shrugged. "Probably good you chose the who as I don't actually have definitive whys. And since I can tell from your tomato complexion that you're angry, and that there's no way you'll darken my door again when your photos are ready in two hours, I'll be the bigger person and run them over to your shop myself."

When we were back on the sidewalk, I glared down at Watson. "I've never been more disappointed in you in my life. You don't like anyone, not really. But the ones you do, have always been some of the nicest people I can imagine. *That* woman made the devil look friendly."

Watson merely stared at me for a moment and then made it clear he was ready to head back across the street, probably to beg a treat from Katie and then fall asleep in the sunshine.

I intended to return to the Cozy Corgi. I *should've* returned to the Cozy Corgi. Watson and I were nearly there, but I veered off at the last second. Between smarting from the interaction with Delilah and my sense of betrayal from Watson, founded or not, if I went back to the bookshop, the only thing I'd accomplish would be pacing around the store and being in a foul mood.

That should've been enough of a clue right there. After nearly four decades on the planet, I had enough self-awareness to know better. When Winifred Page is irritable, frustrated, disgusted, tired, or hungry, she needs a time-out. When she's the marvelous mishmash of all five of those, she needs to take her toys and go home.

But no, I ignored my better judgment and let my ego take over. By the time I stomped into Twin Owl

Scoops, nearly shutting Watson in the door behind me, the smell of fresh-baked waffle cones only served to make me murderous.

There were a few ice cream shops scattered among the businesses of downtown. Most carried a combination of candy and a small offering of baked goods. Petra Yun's ice cream parlor was the oldest in town. It also had the distinction of having the fewest flavors, lackluster décor, and no other options outside of the ice cream variety. If a person wanted sorbet, gelato, or dairy-free, they needed to look elsewhere.

In a town where every store bordered on story-book charm, Twin Owl Scoops was the library book that had been left out in the rain and then shoved through the return slot without being allowed to dry.

It also had the best ice cream anyone had ever tasted in their entire lives. And those homemade waffle cones? I doubted even Katie could concoct a recipe that could compare.

Proving that the unattractive little gem of a store wasn't a secret, despite it being before lunchtime, the line of tourists waiting for their ice cream cones wound around the perimeter of the shop walls.

"May I try a sample of the chocolate and the vanilla?" A hipster with a beard that reached his flannel-covered navel tapped the glass of the display.

Alex looked at the tourist with wide eyes. Petra went through employees at an astonishing rate, but Alex had managed to survive for quite a while. "Um... we're not allowed to give samples, actually. But the vanilla tastes like vanilla, and the chocolate like... chocolate."

"That seems a little unaccommodating." The hipster scowled. "Okay, then, what about the double chocolate?"

Alex shook his head. "I can't get samples of that one either."

"I know that." Hipster tourist sounded like that should have been obvious. "I meant, how does the double chocolate compare to the regular chocolate?"

On any other occasion, the expression on Alex's face would've made me laugh. He was a sweet little guy, though always nervous. He'd been into the bookshop several times; he had a penchant for Regency romances. "Well... the double chocolate tastes like the regular chocolate, except... twice as chocolaty." Starting to sweat, he glanced at the long line of waiting tourists. Petra was notorious for only having one employee work at a time, no matter what the season. Alex's eyes met mine, and he smiled, probably equating a familiar face to salvation. He waved. "Hey!"

The entire line of tourists looked back at me, every single expression making it clear that if I thought I was cutting, there would be bloodshed.

I'd like to see them try.

Hipster man had the same expression on his face, and then his brows knitted as he glanced at Watson. "I don't think you're supposed to have dogs in here."

The entire store was awash with red.

"Here! One second." Alex brought the man's attention back to him and thrust a full-size metal spoon with a heaping portion of ice cream on it at the man. "Try the vanilla. It's my favorite." Apparently Alex decided facing Petra's wrath over giving samples was preferable to watching me turn into a fire-breathing monster.

And yet, did I listen to my better judgment? Did I heed the clear and obvious warnings? Did I pay any attention to the rebuking chuff of my corgi?

"Is Petra in today, Alex?"

He shook his head, but his gaze flicked toward the back.

Leaving my place in line, I marched through the store, only to be halted when Watson didn't follow. I turned with a glare. "Come on."

He glared back. Watson was stubborn in typical corgi fashion, but like the double-chocolate ice cream, he'd gotten his second dose of that particular quality. Typically, I found it charming and, since I had that same characteristic, relatable. In that moment, however, it only added to my resentment of him.

And being aware it was ridiculous that I was feeling resentful of my dog only made it worse. "I. Said. Come. On."

"Fred, I don't think Petra wants to be—" Alex quit talking when I flashed him a look.

I turned back to Traitor McTraitorson. "*Watson.*"

After a few more seconds of his chocolate-eyed glare, Watson acquiesced and followed, his nose lifted in regal aloofness.

And *another* sure sign of impending doom that I ignored. I never won a standoff with Watson. Ever. Not without copious amounts of pleading or bribery with snacks.

Strolling behind the counter, and probably sending the hipster into an aneurysm at the level of my health code violations, I knocked on the office door, waited perhaps a tenth of a second, and walked in.

Petra looked up from behind her desk, where she was typing on an old computer the size of a small icebox. Her eyes went wide with shock. "What in the—" They flicked to Watson, then back to me, hardening. "Are you kidding me right now?"

Looked like I wasn't the only one in a bad mood. This was going to be fun. Petra, though she'd seemed timid when we'd first met, was difficult on a good day. Although, I was the one storming in uninvited to someone's office, not Petra.

She stood before I could get a word out, despite her diminutive size and aged face, and tilted her chin defiantly at me, similar to what Watson had done moments before. "Fred, in case you didn't notice, we're in the height of tourist season and we're a tad busy. I have no doubt as to why you're here, and I simply don't have the time for it."

I glanced around. "I don't see any tourists in here. It's not like you're out front helping Alex." My condescending tone cut through some of my anger. Maybe I was frustrated at the turn of events with Branson and me, reminded of my ex-husband, Garrett, with Pete's affair, or affairs, apparently, and thoroughly revolted by Delilah, but none of that was Petra's fault. I needed to take a step back. I wanted to find who killed Melody and hurt Paulie, and I wanted to do it in record time to rub it in Branson's face, but not at the cost of acting like someone I couldn't respect.

Her lips thinned. "You run your business how you see fit, and I'll run mine. If you want to take in every stray off the street to work in your little book-shop, be my guest."

I bristled at the reference to the twins, and all notions of getting hold of myself vanished. "You don't have time? Really? Isn't Paulie your friend? You two are in the bird club together. Is whatever you're doing more important than trying to find out who tried to kill him? Who murdered Melody?"

Undaunted, Petra managed to stand a little straighter. "Your arrogance is astounding, Winifred Page. You moved to town and instantly start accusing everyone of murdering everyone else. It was only a few months ago you stormed into Alice's candle shop basically accusing both of us of killing Henry. Even made comments about her son. And we were entirely innocent."

I laughed; I couldn't help myself. "Really? You were entirely innocent? Should we call Leo and ask about that illegal owl you had?"

"That's hardly the same thing as murder." Her beautiful complexion went splotchy in her anger, and her tone dipped to cold ice. "What is it now? Going store-to-store pointing fingers and pretending like you're the police again? Tell me, why do you think I did it? Paulie's stupid dogs broke in one night and ate all my ice cream?" At the mention, she looked at Watson. "Like I said, you can have whatever strays you want in your shop, but I run a clean business. Your mutt needs to go."

My head literally throbbed from the pressure of my fury. It didn't matter if I was frustrated with Watson, the way she spoke about him was nearly more than I could handle. "I didn't think you hurt Paulie. You hadn't even entered my mind, despite your personality. But your name came up as someone who was a person of interest. So, you should ask yourself why others in town think you capable of murder. And being so defensive only makes the possibility more feasible."

"Person of interest?" Petra laughed, mimicking me, then plopped back down in her chair. "There you go, being your arrogant self again. Person of interest. You sell *books*, Winifred. You're not the police. And you think because you listen to all the gossip in this little bitty town, that makes you a detective?" She leaned forward, propping her elbows on top of her desk and folding her hands together. "Tell you what, let me give you the rundown on exactly how I feel about Paulie and Melody. But I'll tell you this, as soon as you walk out that door, I'm calling the police, not that they're capable of much, as evidenced by how many murders we've had lately, or that you're still roaming the streets. But I'm not putting up with your entitled harassment again. Once was enough."

"I've never harassed you, not even for—"

"Shut up."

Despite my indignation at her murderous glare, I did.

"No, Paulie and I are *not* friends. However, he's one of the Feathered Friends Brigade, so he's one of my brood. Beyond that, he helped me get my sweet albino golden macaws, Ra and Horus. Though we might not be friends, for that alone, I'd nearly take a bullet for the weird little man." Though she'd started off quiet, her volume rose slightly as she continued. "And I'm not surprised that my name came up as far as Melody Pitts is concerned. I hated that woman alive, and that hasn't changed since she died. She and her spineless husband live next door, and one of her cats came over and killed Azure, my Indian Ringneck. Who ever heard of having seven cats." She rolled her eyes. "Excuse me, soon to be *nine* cats. But while I'll never forgive her, she and her husband paid for my golden macaws in recompense, so debts have been paid."

She was speaking so rapidly I struggled to keep up, and it took me a few seconds to realize an Indian Ringneck was some type of bird.

Petra kept going, a smile beginning to form on her lips as she spoke. "And just because I'm learning I dislike you to the same level of Melody, I'll give you this little gem for free—even though I hate to turn on one of my fellow Feathered Friends Brigade members, but imagine what it would be like to be married to a woman who was so cat obsessed that she chose to fill your home with nasty little feline after nasty little feline even though she knew you were allergic, even though you had to get weekly shots to be able to breathe from all the disgusting cat dander."

I blinked, once more trying to catch up. "Jared is allergic to cats?"

"You are about as quick as slow-churned ice cream, Fred." Her smile blossomed fully as she leaned back in her chair and moved her folded hands to her lap. "I'll make sure when I call the police to let them know that Jared Pitts is the next on your list to be harassed."

In the wake of her ice-cold anger, some of my own had dissipated, ushering in a humiliating fresh wave of embarrassment at how I'd handled myself. "Petra... I—"

"Oh my Lord, you sound like you're going to apologize." Her nostrils flared as if she smelled something sour. "Don't. You'll only go down in my estimation, which can't fall much lower. Just let me say that I hope you soon get taken down a peg or two. You're obnoxious, arrogant, entitled, and altogether insufferable."

Watson let out a low rumble of a growl.

Petra sneered at him. "Try me, mutt. I'll drown you in a flea bath."

Watson continued his growl, and it showed just how on the verge of losing my sanity I was that I felt tears sting behind my eyes at his defense.

I wasn't going to apologize, and I for sure wasn't about to let Petra Yun see me cry. So, I turned, left the office, and strode past the unending line of ice cream craving tourists, with Watson by my side.

ELEVEN

"What a day! We hit the ground running and never stopped." Katie paused from rolling out dough on the marble slab to gesture at the bakery's empty display cases. "Completely sold out, again."

I pulled a chair to the counter, plopped down, and rested my elbow to prop my head. "Yeah, we did pretty good downstairs as well. Thank goodness for Ben. I was utterly useless, what time I was actually here."

"You're not kidding." She grimaced. "Not about the you being useless part. But if it weren't for Nick, I'd have to stay here all night baking. That, or get up at one in the morning to start. But with him helping out, we've got it covered." Katie patted the speckled brown dough and pulled out a large dog bone cookie cutter.

"What are you making?"

She waggled the cookie cutter in my direction. "You really must be as tired as you look if you can't put these clues together."

"I don't think I can put *any* clues together. I'm getting nowhere besides burning bridges with every shop owner in town."

"Fred." Katie took on a placating tone. "It's barely been more than twenty-four hours. Cut yourself a break."

Twenty-four hours? It felt like a week since walking into Paulie's shop and finding him and Melody. How could I be that exhausted after just a day? I focused on the easily solvable mystery. "If you have that much to bake for business tomorrow, why are you making those right now?"

"Because we're out, and after seeing that adorable picture of you two from Delilah's, I decided Watson deserved a treat. Freshly baked."

At Katie speaking his favorite word, Watson exploded up from his napping position in the corner of the bakery and ran toward her.

She grinned down at him and shook her head. "Sorry, buddy. I didn't mean to get you excited. Soon, though, they'll be ready soon."

He whimpered.

"Goodness, if you're going to give me those eyes,

I have no choice." Katie tore off a bit of the excess dough left in between two of the cutout bone shapes and tossed it to him. "There you go. Don't tell your mom."

I forced a laugh. "Go ahead. He deserves it. He's had to put up with one grumpy mother all day. It's not right to punish him because he apparently thinks Delilah hung the moon."

"Really?" Katie stared down at Watson, then back up at me. "The list is growing. Your stepdad, Leo, Ben, and now *Delilah* of all people."

"Well...." I sighed. "No, it wasn't nearly to that level. He didn't actually act like she hung the moon or anything. He was just content to let her pet him and receive her attention. None of the attitude he normally gives to people."

"This is the last one until they're baked." Katie tossed him another piece of dough and then narrowed her eyes as she thought. "You know, when you went to visit Paulie this afternoon, Leo popped by for a snack. I showed him the pictures of you and Watson, and we started talking about Delilah. I filled him in on what you told me." She narrowed her eyes further. "I'm going to want *a lot* more details on that, by the way. Anyway, I was saying how despicable she was, and he got weirdly quiet. To the point that I wondered if he had a past with her."

At that, I sat up straight, wide-awake once more. "No! Absolutely not. He's much too good for her."

"That's what I was thinking, but of course didn't say so."

Katie's response caught my attention. The more time that passed, the more I wondered if the two of them really were having a secret relationship. She didn't sound jealous, just more appalled.

"Finally, I asked him why he was being weird." Katie kept going before I could give it any more consideration. "Turns out the man-eater is quite the animal lover, especially dogs. She has three rescued basset hounds at home. And Leo said that she gives ten percent of all her profits to dog rescues, so, of course, that covers a whole multitude of wrongs in Leo's book."

"Really?" I stared at Watson, who'd fallen asleep once more under his favorite table. Maybe that's all it was. Perhaps Watson could sense Delilah was a dog fanatic. He did seem to pick up on things, and I doubted he was overly concerned about human wedding vows. I felt doubly horrible for being so irritated with him. The other part of Katie's story clicked, and I refocused on her. "Wait a minute. You saw the pictures?"

She looked puzzled for a moment, then realization dawned. "Oh, right, she delivered them right before Leo came in. Ben brought the packet up to me. He didn't tell you before he and Nick left?"

I shook my head.

"I completely forgot about giving it to you with how crazy we were at the end of the day." She dusted off her hands on her apron, then bent to dig below the counter before standing once more and thrusting a flat paper bag at me. "They really came out spectacularly. You look stunning."

Figuring that Katie was just being kind, although typically she was rather blunt, I slipped the tin photographs out of the bag. The smooth metal was cold on my fingertips, and I stared down at the images in surprise. Katie was right. The photos were rather wonderful. Somehow, despite my growing abhorrence of her during the photoshoot, Delilah had captured some moment where I didn't look disgusted. In fact... Katie was right about that too. I looked good; the 1920s style suited me. And Watson.... My heart melted at the sight of him and his little dapper hat and tie, a huge grin over his face as his tongue lolled out. Though I'd paid plenty for the three metal prints, I couldn't help but feel like she'd given me a gift. It was rare that I got a good photo of Watson, let alone with the two of us together. He was not a fan of cameras.

"Oh, sweetie." Katie reached across the counter and squeezed my forearm. "Why are you crying?"

I hadn't even realized I was. But sure enough, I wiped away tears. "I'm just tired. Exhausted for some reason, with no sleep last night and then today's been... well, a day. And this... it's wonderful."

"Oh." Katie released my forearm and shrugged. "I'd hoped it was because you realized you needed to give up on your ridiculous broomstick skirts of every drab earth-tone color available and switch styles to something a little more...." She flicked her fingers at the pictures, apparently at a loss for words, which was maybe a first for her.

I threw back my head and laughed. Boy, didn't that feel good, and needed. "Of course that's what you would say." No wonder she was my best friend as well as my business partner. "So, you think I should start dressing as a flapper girl on a daily basis?"

"It would be an improvement." Her mutter was just low enough to be heard, and the corner of her lips turned up in a wicked grin.

I swatted at her. "You're awful!"

"No, that would be your fashion taste."

"I'm not sure you have any room to talk. You're the one wearing a T-shirt with Pokémon characters underneath that apron."

"And proud of it." Katie chuckled as she transferred the bone-shaped biscuits to a baking tray. "But we're treading on dangerous territory here." Her smile grew a touch more serious. "How was Paulie when you visited him this afternoon?"

"Better." The reminder caused my spirits to lift nearly as much as the laughter. "They moved him up to stable and think that he'll wake up sooner rather than later. So at least he's not quite fighting for his life like he was. But they're still saying we won't know the extent of the damage to his brain, if any, until he wakes."

"Thank God. I thought he was looking better when I went to see him this morning." Katie wiped a tear from her eye and left a smudge of flour behind. "Was Athena there? Leo and I are supposed to trade shifts with her later this evening."

"Yeah. She came in just as I was leaving. Officer Jackson was there too. I think they're using him to guard Paulie as a way to help him ease back into returning to work."

"Good. I hope he's still there when Leo and I go later. Maybe I should make some lemon bars real quick as well to take to him." She shook her head. "I can't believe he almost died for you and me." She cleared her throat and then looked at me meaningfully. "So... no Branson?"

I shook my head.

"No call either?"

I shook my head again. "No. But honestly, that's a good thing. I'm completely off my game today. If he called, I'd jump down his throat again and make it a million times worse. Just like I have with everyone else I've interacted with." I'd replayed the scene with Petra on a continuous loop, and every single time was a touch more embarrassing. She hadn't been pleasant either, but I couldn't blame her. I'd stormed into her business on the warpath. She had every right to treat me the way she had. I was planning on going to her sometime during the next day or two, once I was rested and knew I was under better control to apologize.

Clearly Katie could read my mind. "You've got to quit beating yourself up. Our friend is in the hospital fighting for his life, and you walked in on *another* dead body yesterday. Your boyfriend—" She raised her hand as I started to protest. "—or whatever he was... or... is... pulled a Jekyll and Hyde out of the blue. You're trying to save the day once more, and on top of all that, you barely got an ounce of sleep last night. You don't have to be perfect, nor do you have to be pleasant all the time. It doesn't sound like any of the three people you talked to today were overly pleasant themselves, either in attitude or deed."

Her defense of me helped somewhat. She wasn't entirely wrong, though she wasn't entirely right either. I didn't care about the reason. I expected more of myself than that. "You're good at the best-friend role, Katie Michelle Pizzolato."

"As are you, Winifred Wendy Page." She winked, then carried the tray of dog treats to the oven, slid them in, and set the timer before dusting off her hands once more and returning to the counter. "So... fill me in. You still haven't told me whatever it was you said you'd found out about Jared."

Jared! I'd been so busy being angry, then worrying about Paulie, and then doing round after round in the boxing ring with my embarrassment and guilt as I helped tourists with books, I'd completely forgotten.

I matched Katie's posture, leaning over like two

busybodies. "According to Petra, Jared is allergic to cats."

Katie scrunched up her face, started to speak, then scrunched up her face some more. Then she reached into a pile of papers by the cash register and pulled out the Belvedere and Cameo announcement. "You're telling me the man who lives with a cotillion of cats is allergic? How is that possible? Surely Petra's wrong. If that were true, you'd have walked in on *his* dead body yesterday, thanks to anaphylactic shock, not Melody's."

"You're awful." I swatted at her again, but I couldn't suppress a chuckle. "Apparently, he takes weekly allergy shots."

"Really? That's... I don't even know what that is. That's insane." Katie blinked, clearly baffled. "Why would he do that?"

I shrugged. "I don't know. I suppose, if the cats were important enough to Melody, he did it for her, or he's just as cat obsessed as she was." The memory from the day before flickered through my mind. "He must be. The cat palace that Melody bought had a big bow on it yesterday and a gift tag with Jared's name. Maybe he loves them so much his allergies don't matter."

"Now *that's* love, whether for his wife or for the cats, like real get-you-committed kind of love."

"Yeah... you're right." I thought back to Petra's tirade. "The way Petra presented it made it sound like it was a reason Jared might've killed his wife."

Katie started to shake her head, then paused. "I was about to say I couldn't see him doing that, that the two of them really seemed in love, but I don't know them that well, and if he really is allergic to cats, I can't say I blame him. I'm not even allergic, and if someone forced me to live with nine Persian cats, I'd murder them too."

"The cats or the person?"

"All of the above!"

I laughed again at the expression on her face.

She grinned, but her tone was serious. "I'm not kidding. That sounds like the seventh layer of hell. Actually, the *ninth* layer of hell." She propped one hand on the counter and the other on her hip. "Although, that doesn't explain why he'd hurt Paulie. If he was going to kill Melody, he could just do it at home. Smother her with hairballs or something."

Though I could tell she was trying to make me laugh, she had a thought. "Well... I suppose if she was getting the cats from Paulie, and Jared does have feelings about it, then maybe he'd be angry at Paulie as well?"

Katie considered, then shook her head. "I don't know. That seems a little far-fetched. But again, so does living with nine cats, so... sure. In this case, it makes perfect sense."

"I just don't think so, though. You should've heard him yesterday. The reaction he had wasn't fake when he found Melody's body. It couldn't have been."

"Maybe it was guilt?" Katie didn't sound convinced by her own suggestion. "Maybe he's who you should talk to next."

The thought gave me a sick feeling in my stomach. It was one thing to talk to people who were on the sidelines of the whole thing. It was another to think about questioning a man who seemed to truly love his dead wife.

My phone rang, cutting off the thought. I glanced down out of habit, not intending to answer, but sat up straighter with a little jolt when I saw Branson's name on the display.

I tilted it so Katie could see when she gave me a quizzical expression. Her eyes widened.

"Right? Tell me about it." Though part of me

demanded I let it go to voicemail, I stood, wanting to get it over with. "This could go so many ways."

"I bet he's calling to apologize for how he spoke to you last." Despite her words, Katie didn't sound convinced.

Though I hoped on the off chance she was right, I knew she wasn't. I was willing to bet Petra had followed through and called the police the second I'd left her office. And, honestly, I couldn't blame her.

"I'm gonna take this, I'll be right back."

"'K. I'll start the lemon bars for Officer Jackson."

I gave her a thumbs-up as I hit Accept and headed toward the stairs leading to the bookshop to speak in private. "Hello? Branson?" So far so good, my tone sounded passably calm and at ease.

"Fred." Even just saying my name, Branson sounded far from calm and at ease. More like tense and angry. Any hope I'd had of this going smoothly flew out the window.

"How are you?"

Branson bypassed the question. "We discussed this last night. I couldn't have made myself any clearer."

Unlike my reaction the night before, after beating myself up for the way I'd interacted with Petra, guilt sliced through me at his words. Still, I wanted to be sure and not give away too much if I didn't have to. "I take it you heard from Petra?"

"Sure did."

Nope. He didn't sound calm or at ease in the slightest. "I admit, I didn't handle things very well with her this afternoon. I lost my temper."

Branson paused on the other end of the line. He'd probably been expecting an argument. When he spoke again, his tone was a little softer. "She's filing a restraining order. But if you'll agree to stay away from her, I'll see if I can talk her out of it."

"What!" Now I sounded tense and angry. "Are you serious? I didn't threaten her. A restraining order? That's insanity!"

"Okay, then...." Branson sighed, probably expelling any of the softness he had left. "Let's try this again. I'll try to talk her out of it if—"

"Talk her out of it?" For what had to have been the billionth time that day, my temper became a living entity. "Let her file. It's not going to go through. It makes no sense. All she's trying to do is make a point, to cause me a headache as payback."

"Did you or did you not go into her office, uninvited, with your dog, and accuse her of murder?"

"No! Of course I didn't. I...." *Dang it!* "Well, I

didn't accuse her of murder, exactly. Not in so many words."

Branson groaned. "So much for me talking her out of it. Fred, let me reiterate if I wasn't clear enough last night. Stay out of this. It's none of your business. If you do, I'll try to help you with this. If you don't, then not only will I not protect you from legal action, I'll file the paperwork myself."

Much to my irritation, that sliced through my anger once more, leaving me feeling something so much worse. Hurt and a sense of betrayal. "Why are you doing this?"

"Because...." His voice wavered, and in that slight hiccup, I heard the real Branson or at least who I thought was the real Branson. "It's just my job." Then it was gone, returned back to the hard cold stone. "So, let me do it, and you stick to doing yours."

I hung up on him.

At the snuffling on the other side of the door of my cabin, Watson and I paused on the porch. "Who knows what we are about to walk into. The monsters might've destroyed our home. Maybe I should've locked them in the dog run to be on the safe side." I glanced down at Watson in commiseration but halted at the sight of his big brown eyes staring up at me. I knelt and took his sweet, foxlike face into my hands and dipped my head to press our foreheads together. "I'm sorry I was so irritable today."

Watson chuffed, darted his tongue out to lick his nose and managed to get mine as well.

I laughed but didn't pull back, needing the close contact with him more than I'd realized. "I'm going to pretend that was a kiss of forgiveness and not your version of spitting on me." I stroked his cheeks with my thumbs for a few more seconds. "I really am sorry. I don't know why I felt so betrayed by you. You're allowed to like whoever you do for any reason."

Speaking those words out loud clarified what should have been obvious. Though I hadn't been sure where Branson and I were headed... No... that wasn't true. I'd been fairly certain where Branson and I were headed. I just didn't know the when or how fast we would get there. But now... I was back to not being sure where Branson and I were headed. No, that also wasn't true. I did know, but the destination had changed, and I was surprised how much it hurt, how much it triggered old emotions from the past, from my marriage, from the divorce, and all those years between.

I pulled back slightly so I could look into Watson's eyes. "Here I am doing therapy on the porch with my dog. You must think I'm crazy."

Watson tilted his head in that adorable dog fashion. His thoughts were clear. *The only thing that would make you crazy, lady, is if you thought I didn't already know you were crazy.*

"You're not wrong." Chuckling, I kissed the tip of his nose. "I am sorry. I love you desperately. Forgive me?"

He whined, which I wanted to pretend meant

*Of course I forgive you. I love you more than anything in the entire universe.* But knowing Watson, the smart money was on *You already hung out too long at the shop with Katie, and now we're killing time on the porch. Do you realize how late we are for dinner?*

"And again, you're not wrong." I stood and unlocked the door, bracing myself. "Here goes nothing." It didn't matter if the house was destroyed. I'd lost my temper for the last time that day, no matter what.

Sure enough, as I opened the door, insanity met Watson and me in the form of two chunky, tongue-lolling, hyperactive corgis slamming into my legs and into Watson's face with frantic joy.

Watson growled, reminding them he was the king of *this* particular castle, and then moved aside.

For my part, I turned the deadbolt, and then sank to the floor and let Flotsam and Jetsam cover me in puppy kisses and affection. By the time Watson joined in, though with much more reserve and class, we had a practical tornado of corgi hair swirling around us.

On the far side of the room, I noticed a destroyed stuffed alligator.

Whatever. That had been Watson's least favorite

toy anyway. From what I could tell, the rest of the
house was intact.

As I cooked a gargantuan baked sweet potato for
myself and chicken breasts for the dogs, having to
watch every step I made to keep from tripping over
the corgi herd at my feet, I mentally examined, then
set aside every hurt, frustration, and unanswered
question from the past twenty-four hours or so. By
the time I curled up on the armchair with my new
*Port Danby* novel, with the windows of the house
letting in the cool July night breeze so the blaze in
the fireplace didn't suffocate us, I almost felt like
myself. The surround-sound effect of the staggered
corgi snores didn't hurt either.

By the time dawn broke gently through the bedroom
curtains, sleep had worked the remaining magic over
any of the areas not attended to by Watson, Flotsam,
and Jetsam.

There was a moment of regret for some of my
behavior the day before, but I shut that off. Regret
did nothing. It was a new day, and I would do better.
And in retrospect, I hadn't done anything out of line
during my conversation with Pete Miller. Delilah
Johnson hadn't been able to read my thoughts about

her, though she probably had from my expression. I didn't owe her an apology, but I could drop in to thank her for the lovely photographs. Maybe buy one of her overpriced frames for one of them. As far as Petra Yun? Well... I *did* owe her an apology, and I probably needed to do it quickly before I got served with a restraining order or whatever she was planning to file against me. If not, I'd get myself arrested by receiving a restraining order and then calling her up to tell her I was sorry.

Although, that was going to take some thought. How did a person apologize for their behavior while not apologizing for wondering if the other party had recently committed murder?

I'd have to ask Katie to google it.

After breakfast, with coffee in my hand, I affixed leashes to all three dogs' collars and prepared for a morning walk. It wasn't routine, as Watson was with me every step of the day and got walked constantly. But I figured Flotsam and Jetsam were probably desperate for one. Besides, not only was it good for them, but if they burned off some energy, it might save the rest of Watson's stuffed animals from impending death. Though, I'd put his favorite yellow duck on the shelf, so it was safe.

I needed to figure out how to get the twosome

their own toys. That would probably make them feel better.

We barely made it off the porch before I realized I lacked the skill to drink my coffee while managing three dog leashes, two of which were whipping around like seaweed caught in a typhoon. With a small sense of loss, I placed the coffee on the porch, promising to microwave it and let it fulfill its caffeinated purpose as soon as we arrived back home.

I hadn't walked in the forest surrounding my house very much. I'd simply enjoyed it from the cozy spot on the driftwood bench on my porch. I needed to make it more of a habit—as we walked, greater and greater peace came over me. Being surrounded by the tall evergreens and groves of aspen and sheltered by the ragged peaks above us offered a sense of protection. The aromas of pine and earth mingled with the crunch of twigs and scrape of rock underfoot and contrasted beautifully with the gurgling of the rushing river nearby. Purple-and-white columbine and blue flax lined the path, reminding me that I truly did live in paradise. The only thing missing was the scamper of chipmunks, songs of birds, and stumbling upon an elk around the bend. I was certain all those creatures were near but staying well out of sight with Flotsam and Jetsam doing a spectacular job of making our presence known.

The coffee was lukewarm by the time we made it back to the porch, and as I dug the keys out of the pocket of my skirt, a flash of white caught my attention within the trees on the other side of the house. It only took me a moment to identify the spiky, feathery hair of Myrtle Bantam.

Though I'd never seen her in the area around my home, I had no doubt why she was there. I was also certain she wanted to be alone. But she'd been on my list to speak to, though nowhere near the top. I decided to take the opportunity. Shutting Flotsam and Jetsam safely back inside, I gathered up Watson and my coffee, and we strode toward the owner of Wings of the Rockies.

Myrtle was so caught up staring through her binoculars into the trees she didn't notice us coming, which gave me a chance to observe. As ever, the thin, bony woman reminded me of a crane, and was nearly as birdlike in her sudden, jerky manners as the feathered fowls she devoted her life to.

As we approached, I started to warn Watson to be as quiet as possible. I stepped on a twig, snapping it in half, and decided to keep my advice to myself.

Myrtle didn't look over at the noise, but kept her

attention focused as she readjusted some setting on the binoculars. "Come here, Fred. You need to see this." Typically, Myrtle's voice had an intense squawking quality, but her whisper was little more than a chirp.

I closed the distance between us. Before I offered a greeting, she shoved the binoculars into my hands and pointed to the uppermost branch of a juniper. Taking them, I aimed them in the direction she indicated but didn't see anything more than a close-up of the pine needles.

"Here, let me take Watson's leash." She slid it free from my hand and then whispered in my ear, "It's close to where that branch is severed, appears to have been a lightning strike."

I looked over the top of the binoculars, located the burn mark, then readjusted accordingly. After a few seconds of weaving around, I found it. A bird, of course. It looked a little larger than a robin, if I wasn't mistaken. Mostly a soft gray with a white throat and belly, with black striping around the eyes and over the wings and tail. The head almost looked too large for its body. As if it knew I was watching, it transformed from sleek and raptor-like to a ball of fluff as it shimmied its feathers and then turned sleek once more—transitioning from beautiful to cute and back again. "It's lovely. What is it?" I didn't know one species of bird from the next, outside of those everyone knew, but I was certain Myrtle wanted to explain.

"I'm almost certain it's a *San Clemente* loggerhead shrike." Her hushed tone held excitement. "It's a subspecies out of the loggerhead shrikes. In 1996, there were only fifteen of those in the wild and only ten in captivity. A decade later, there were forty breeding pairs in the wild. Though we've still got a ways to go with it, that little fellow is a shining example of why bird conservation is so important."

"He's... beautiful." I looked for another descriptor but couldn't find anything more specific. He was pretty, but outside of colors and size, I didn't really recognize the difference between most birds. "I don't think I've seen him before." Like I'd know.

"Of course you haven't." She snagged the binoculars back and looked again for herself as she spoke. "They're from the San Clemente Island in California, obviously."

*Obviously*. "Cool." Again, I wasn't really sure what I was supposed to say. "Wonder what he's doing here."

Myrtle peered over at me from the binoculars,

offering an approving smile. "Exactly, Winfred. Exactly."

"Well, the town is full of human tourists right now. Maybe it's bird tourist season too."

The look of approval faded.

"Or... maybe not." At that moment, I wasn't a thirty-nine-year-old woman who owned a bookstore, who'd been a professor and was highly educated. I was back in fourth grade and had just received a withering stare from Mrs. Weser. I sipped my coffee to assure myself I was no longer in grade school.

Myrtle looped the strap of the binoculars over her head and around her neck then let them fall to her chest as she looked at me fully. "If I'm right, and it is the San Clemente variety, while it's wonderful to see and there's a chance that it somehow flew here on its own—though that would be unusual—it begs the question, *why* is it here?" She bugged her eyes out at me as if she was sharing some scandalous piece of gossip. "It's a bit of a mystery, and it's got me worried."

It only took me a couple of seconds to catch up. "You think there's more poaching and illegal trading of birds going on? Maybe this one escaped."

Again, her expression said that was obvious. "That never stops, and it never will. Poaching and the illegal animal trade will be a constant battle, but it's one we must fight." She nodded sagely. "I'll need to get Leo's opinion on it."

I figured that was about as good of a segue as I was going to get. "Speaking of birds that people aren't supposed to own...."

Myrtle groaned and shook her head. "Say no more. I heard all about it at last night's Feathered Friends Brigade Meeting." She reached out a knobby hand and patted my shoulder. "I'm still kicking myself for changing my mind and letting Petra rejoin the bird club after what she did. But I told myself it would be better to keep an eye on her that way. But, goodness, she's high-maintenance."

Her touch threw me off. I wasn't exactly Myrtle's favorite person during my first several weeks in Estes, and though we'd bonded months before, I still wasn't used to her moments of affection for me. "I forgot bird club was last night. Was Jared there?"

And we were back to that reproachful look. "Of course not. The man just lost his wife. Although...." She seemed to consider it. "He's one of the more devoted members of the bird club that I've had in a while. I suppose it wouldn't have surprised me if he'd come after all, for comfort and normality if nothing else." Her eyes narrowed, but

I didn't see judgment. "You don't suspect Jared, do you?"

After the day before, it was a relief to have her simply accept that I was looking into things and not question it. "Honestly, at this point I have no clue. And I don't know him at all, but I keep getting strange details about him."

Her head perked in that birdlike manner of hers. "Really? Anything I should be concerned about?" Her gray eyes darted toward the... whatever kind of bird it was, then back to me. "Do you think he's infiltrating the bird club for nefarious reasons?"

I couldn't help but laugh. "No. I haven't heard much about him in relationship to birds, actually. More about cats."

Looking relieved, Myrtle nodded. "Oh, his allergies."

I flinched. "So, it is true. Jared's allergic to cats?"

"Oh yes. The poor boy has to take allergy shots, pills, and the whole thing. I don't know how he does it. Supposedly the allergies are fairly severe." She sniffed, emotion washing over her features. "The only thing the man seemed to love more than birds was his wife. And she always struck me as rather selfish by expecting him to live with all those cats." She shuddered.

"Petra didn't seem overly fond of Melody either."

Myrtle's squawked laugh was so sharp that she clamped her hand over her mouth and checked to see whether the bird was still there. It was. "You can say that again. Though she's no fan of Jared either. I'm certain she sees him as an accomplice to the death of her beautiful Indian Ringneck. Not that I blame her for being upset, obviously." She lowered her voice again, clearly indicating that the next bit was most definitely salacious. "Although, even if Petra wouldn't admit it, I think she's actually rather glad it happened. After all, she now has two albino golden macaws, and those don't come cheap. Although, Leo, Paulie, and I made sure she got them through legal means this time, I promise you that."

That much of Petra's story lined up at least.

Watson had been sniffing around our feet, and apparently was feeling ignored, as he pressed his cold nose to the thin strip of flesh revealed between Myrtle's ankle socks and her too-short jeans, causing her to jump.

In another act I wasn't accustomed to, since she used to look at Watson in the same way she spoke about cats, Myrtle bent down and stroked over Watson's head and back. "Well, hello, sweet one. I was so enraptured I didn't notice you. How's my little hero?"

Though not exuberant like he was with Barry, Leo, and Ben, he offered her an affectionate lick, accepted her attention for a few more moments and then wandered away once more.

She smiled after him and stood. "What do you think? I can see the wheels turning."

"I think that's part of what's throwing me off. Paulie, that is." As Myrtle had been petting Watson, I replayed her last comments about Paulie helping her and Leo make sure the birds Petra procured were legal. "What's the connection between Paulie and Melody? It's got to be birds or cats, right? If the connection is cats, then it points to Jared. If it's birds, it points to Petra."

"Yes, I can see what you mean." She glanced away, a strange expression crossing her face.

"Okay, now I can see *your* wheels turning. What is it?"

She shook her head. "I'm not one to give in to gossip. Unless it's bird related, and I don't think this one is."

"Myrtle, if it's something that could help figure out who hurt Paulie, who murdered Melody, I don't know if your aversion to gossip should get in the way."

"You're right, of course." She gave a sharp shake of her head as if making up her mind. "I just feel like I'm betraying him, but maybe I'm not. When I went to visit Paulie yesterday, it killed me seeing that he was being guarded by the police, as if they're worried that whoever it was will try again." She didn't wait for me to respond, leveling her gaze once more, determined. "I don't know what it means, but I'm wondering if it's not bird or cat related. Paulie's been acting very strange the past week. I'm sure you've noticed."

"Have you seen him with a woman too?"

"A woman?" Her eyes widened in understanding. "Oh... well, that would explain what was going on. A secret relationship." She smiled, suddenly wistful. "That's lovely. He's such a lonely man most of the time. It would be nice for him to find someone. Maybe that's all it was, the beginning of a new, secret relationship. Perhaps I just misjudged his excitement for worry."

It seemed we kept coming back to that. A strange blonde woman and secret relationships.

As if out of the blue, the memory of observing him with Melody as I stood at the window flitted through my mind. I hadn't known who she was. I'd simply seen him whispering with a blonde woman and then her hugging him. Even I had assumed there was something romantic going on. Though that didn't make sense with what Delilah had said describing some mousy woman. Melody was anything but mousy; she'd been beautiful. Although, maybe by Delilah's standards... who could say?

Wait... No. *Athena* had referred to a mousy-looking blonde woman. I couldn't remember how Delilah had described her, though I knew it wasn't flattering. Surely Athena wouldn't give such an attribute to Melody. Could the two blonde women be one and same?

"Myrtle...." I hated what I was thinking.

"There go your wheels again."

I decided to go for it. "Okay, this is pure gossip that I'm making up on the spot, so go with me for a second, but please don't repeat it as I'm sure it can't be true."

"I've already told you; I don't gossip. Nor do I require such base warnings." She gave me a serious stare but didn't sound overly offended.

"Do you think... do you think Paulie and Melody might have been having an affair?" As soon as I said the words out loud, I rejected them. He wouldn't do that. Even if he had secrets, I believed I'd seen the core of who Paulie was—he was a good man. Plus, Pete was saying that Melody was lecturing him about his own affair. Surely she wouldn't be judging him while having one of her own.

"Absolutely not." Myrtle didn't even waver. "Impossible. I can't speak for Melody, though it seemed like she and Jared had a good marriage, at least from his side of things, but Paulie would *never* do anything of the sort."

"No, of course. You're right. It's just that...." I sighed. "I keep hearing about some mystery blonde, and you said that you've noticed Paulie acting strange like he has a secret. Maybe it would be too easy if it were Melody. It would definitely make a stronger connection than birds or cats on why they would both have been attacked."

She hummed in understanding. "Jared."

I nodded.

Myrtle seemed to consider again. "Maybe. He doesn't seem the type to me, but maybe. Although I simply can't believe Paulie would be having an affair with a married woman."

"No, me neither."

She gripped my forearm again suddenly, excited. "I know! The Feathered Friends Brigade is having a special outing this weekend that Leo's leading, of course. We're going to study birds of prey in the national park. Why don't you come? You can observe some of your suspects in their natural habitat. I'll see if I can talk Jared into it. I bet I can."

It wasn't a bad idea, but then I remembered what paperwork was about to be filed. "I don't think that would be a good idea. Petra and I aren't on the best of terms right now, as it sounds like you heard last night. And I'm afraid she's not completely unjustified. I plan on going by this afternoon and apologizing."

Without missing a beat, Myrtle shook her head. "No, don't do that. I know Petra very well, more than I used to, in any case. That would only stoke the flames of fury. Give her time. If you still feel like you need to apologize later, do it once the matter has calmed down." Myrtle chuckled self-consciously. "I have a confession. Since we're talking about apologies, maybe it's time."

I had to keep from grinning. I knew exactly where she was headed. "Okay."

She glanced away, unusually nervous. "Well... I can't say that I don't partially understand how Petra feels. This may shock you, but... I wasn't exactly fond of you when you first moved to town. And I...

might've... sort of—" She cleared her throat, before finishing in a rush. "—called the police and made an official complaint about you questioning me in my shop, and I *might* have alluded to it being akin to harassment." Her gaze flicked back, embarrassed and full of apology.

"You did?" Again I had to suppress my natural reaction. I'd known. Branson had told me, and we'd shared quite the laugh about it, about her. How things had changed....

The thought threatened to bring a wave of sadness, and I shoved it away.

"I did." Myrtle gripped my hand that time. "And I'm sorry. I was wrong. And so is Petra. Maybe you take some time to get used to, and sometimes you might be a little abrupt or determined, but you're simply trying to make the world a better place. And those very qualities are what helped you save me." She smiled. "I hope you'll forgive me."

Though her arms flapped in what felt like panic, I wrapped Myrtle into a quick hug. "There's no forgiveness needed."

After my early morning birdwatching session with Myrtle, I went to the Cozy Corgi and pretended everything was normal—partly because I was a little gun-shy after the bang-up job I'd done the day before, but also because sometimes I thought more clearly when my hands and brain were busy doing something else. I hoped the clues and puzzle pieces would jumble together in the back of my mind and snap into place while I worked.

As Watson and I went through the morning routine of getting after-breakfast dessert in the form of a freshly baked almond croissant from Katie—of which Watson got a fourth—and a piping hot dirty chai from Nick—of which Watson got none—no revelation came as to why Jared would attack both his wife and Paulie. Maybe the cat castle had been the final straw piled on top of endless allergy shots, but surely he wouldn't have gone after Paulie for it. Unless there was an affair, which I just couldn't believe.

As I observed Ben make multiple sales of corgi books in the kids' section with Watson hanging out in adoration at his feet, nothing clicked into place with Petra either. From both Myrtle and Petra's own accounts, even if she was angry that the Pitts' cat killed her bird, she'd ended up in a more desirable position with two new, rarer, more expensive parrots. And again, while maybe she was harboring some resentment toward Melody, it made no sense why she'd try to kill Paulie. If there were an affair happening, there was no stretch my imagination could make that would cause Petra to care about it one way or another.

As I introduced customer after customer to their next favorite novel or series, I couldn't fathom who the mysterious blonde seen with Paulie could be. When I thought of her, my gut got that tingle. Somehow she was involved. Had to be. There'd been no whispers of mysterious women in Paulie's life until recently. It couldn't be coincidence that she showed up and Paulie nearly got killed. But still... that made no sense with Melody. Unless.... It sounded like Melody might've had a touch of my personality—

sticking her nose in places others thought it shouldn't go. After all, she *was* trying to talk Pete Miller out of his affair with Delilah. Maybe she was doing the same if Paulie was having an affair with the mystery blonde. That seemed like a stretch too.

No matter how focused I was on the bookshop, no matter how intensely I actively avoided thinking about the possibilities, the puzzle pieces only swirled and came nowhere near forming an image, not even a partial one.

Following the after-lunch rush, just as the midday afternoon showers were about to begin, I told Katie goodbye, grabbed a freshly baked all-natural dog bone treat for Watson and an equally freshly baked lemon bar for myself, left Ben in charge of the bookshop, and drove to the hospital. Maybe something would click there as I looked at Paulie's face and got lost in the beeping of the machines and the smell of antiseptic. Or maybe a miracle would happen, Paulie would wake, sit straight up in bed, look me in the eyes, and announce the whodunit with a flourish.

As I turned my Mini Cooper into the hospital parking lot, I glanced at the blue station wagon at the stop sign waiting to pull out onto the street.

We were probably five yards past the station wagon and into the parking lot when I slammed on the brakes and had to stretch out a protective hand to keep Watson in place. Luckily, there were no cars behind us.

Craning around in my seat, I turned just in time to see the station wagon pull out into traffic and drive away.

That had been Jared Pitts driving the station wagon. I was nearly certain of it.

For a crazy moment, I considered doing a U-turn and chasing him down. The *why* of that notion, I couldn't be sure. Nor did I have any idea what I would do if I caught him. Fear tickled at the possibilities. Maybe he'd been in Paulie's room; finished the job he'd started.

No, Officer Jackson was on guard. Paulie was fine.

Although... Officer Jackson had just returned to the force after a bullet in his brain. Maybe he was still recovering. Maybe he was tired, had fallen asleep, and Jared snuck in to sever loose ends.

I was being crazy. But the possibility, combined with having no idea what to do with Jared once I caught him had me speeding to the parking lot, finding the closest space, and hurrying to the front doors with Watson.

We'd just stepped into the hospital when I paused for a second time. I was so used to Watson going with me everywhere that I hadn't even thought when I'd brought him with me. I was certain dogs weren't allowed in the hospital.

Although, Athena had brought Pearl with her the other day. Of course, that dog hid easily away in her purse, not to mention it would take a brave nurse to stand in Athena's path.

Watson looked up at me questioningly as to why we'd stopped, and I took his hint. I channeled Athena, lifted my chin, strode with purpose and direction to the elevator and straight to Paulie's room where Officer Jackson sat outside the doorway. No one stopped us, which was the good news. The bad news was that Brent Jackson's chin nearly touched his chest as he snored softly.

I didn't bother waking him. I simply rushed into Paulie's room, a sick feeling in the pit of my stomach.

From the other side of Paulie's bed, Athena Rose sat up straight in surprise at my brash entrance as she fluttered her fingers over her chest. "Fred! You nearly gave me a heart attack. What in the world is wrong?"

I glanced from her to Paulie. There was no blood

on the sheets, the beeping of the machines was steady and strong, and if anything, Paulie's complexion was more his typical color than it had been before.

"Fred, you're scaring me."

I finally looked back to Athena. "Paulie is okay?"

With a furrowed crease between her brows, she nodded. "Yes... a little better than when you called this morning. They think he could wake up anytime."

"No... I mean...." I gestured to where I thought the parking lot was. "Jared, I just saw Jared leaving as we pulled in. At least I think it was him."

"Oh, yes, he came to visit." She sat back, clearly relieved. "Very sweet of him, considering what a wreck he was. The man looks at death's door. He didn't stay long but offered his best wishes. Said he'd be praying. It would only be natural for a husband to wonder why his wife was taken and Paulie survived, and Jared didn't seem like that at all. Very sweet indeed."

"He visited Paulie, as in he came in here to see Paulie?"

At that moment, Watson pulled his leash free of my grip, which I must have been holding slack in my surprise, and trotted cheerfully to where Pearl was sitting on Athena's lap.

With a pat on Watson's head, Athena lowered Pearl to the floor so the customary greeting of licking and sniffing could commence. When she looked back up at me, her dark greenish-brown eyes were sharp, her tone more intrigued than surprised. "You suspect Jared. Really...?"

For some reason, I checked Paulie again, as if I didn't trust my own eyesight the first time. "Not necessarily. I don't know who I suspect, but I'm wondering about Jared." I refocused on Athena once more. "Were you in here the whole time with him?"

She nodded, and her voice grew quiet. "You're worried he might have come to hurt Paulie. Keep him from waking up."

"Again, I don't know. It was just a thought. Then I panicked. I'm really off my game lately." Not nearly as much as the day before, but no need to offer examples. As my heart calmed, I walked to the side of Paulie's bed and squeezed his hand. "I do think he looks better."

"Me too. Like I said, the doctors believe he's improving. They say it's nearly miraculous how much the swelling in his brain has already gone down." She sniffed, wiped her eyes, and looked at the dogs, who'd curled up together at her feet. She wasn't an overly emotional or demonstrative woman.

Just seeing Paulie look so much better, combined with the good news did more to soothe me than the full night's sleep I'd gotten. "Miraculous indeed. To get hit in the head that hard and then stabbed by scissors and already improving. We have a lot to be thankful for." Though I'd been looking at Paulie, I felt Athena's gaze and looked over. "What?"

She gave a shrug. "I suppose it doesn't really matter. But Paulie wasn't stabbed with scissors."

"Yes, he was. I saw the weapon myself." I shuddered. "At least the handle of them. I suppose I could've been wrong. Maybe they were dog nail clippers or something with similar handles."

"Melody *was* stabbed with scissors, but not Paulie. He was stabbed with a knife, a big one, apparently." That time she shuddered.

A knife? I hadn't seen a knife anywhere. "Are you sure?"

She nodded. "Yes, I heard Officer Green and Officer Jackson whispering about it a couple of hours ago in the hallway. I figured Sergeant Wexler told you."

No... He most definitely hadn't. There was a squeeze on my hand, causing me to flinch. Then a second one before I realized what was happening. I looked down at my hand in wonder just in time to see the third squeeze. "Athena! Paulie's squeezing my hand."

She got up in a rush, causing the dogs to scramble out of her way, and came to the other side of Paulie's bed. "He did that to me this morning too. I think he knows we're here."

As in reply, he squeezed again.

The tears in my eyes matched Athena's. "Yes. I think somehow he does."

After leaving the hospital, I drove straight to Paulie's. Though I had renewed hope that he would wake soon, there was still no telling how long he'd need to be hospitalized. Athena had asked about how Flotsam and Jetsam were doing, and as I answered, I realized I could've made them feel much more at home than I had, and felt rather ashamed that the idea hadn't occurred to me earlier. The least I could do would be to swing by and pick up their beds and a couple of their favorite toys, bring some of their home into mine.

Though Paulie had become a genuine friend over the past few months, I'd not realized that I'd never been in his home. When he joined Katie, Leo, and me, it was always at a restaurant or at the movies.

Walking through his tiny little home revealed that even though he might have secrets, one of which *could* be an affair with the mystery blonde, I had a good sense of who Paulie Mertz was. Nothing about the decor surprised me at first. The house was messy and cluttered, not dirty, but along the lines of what a person would expect to find in a teenage boy's bedroom. If that teenage boy knew how to operate a vacuum and how to dust. Similarly, toys filled the space. I'd forgotten Paulie had said he'd wanted to open a toyshop when he'd first moved to Estes Park. Though I knew he loved animals, especially his two corgis, it was clear the man was obsessed with toys. The cabinets on either side of his entertainment center in the living room were nothing more than display cases for Star Wars and superhero action figures. All the artwork on the walls was movie posters of the same things.

As soon as we entered his house, Watson tore off, his nose to the ground, having an absolute heyday with the bevy of new smells.

The furniture itself was a mishmash of styles. Actually, style would be a misnomer. If I'd had to guess, I would've placed money that he'd taken a U-

Haul to Goodwill and purchased everything they had all at once. None of it matched, and most of it was a little worse for wear. That part did surprise me a little. I doubted he was going to get rich operating a pet shop in a tourist town, but I was certain he was doing better than the home indicated. Although... I wasn't a toy collector. Maybe they were a lot more expensive than I imagined

It also seemed that he spared no expense spoiling Flotsam and Jetsam, which was to be expected. Dog toys littered the floor. I chose four of them at random and piled them up by the door.

I found both the dog beds, and Watson, in Paulie's bedroom. Even in there, the furniture didn't match, but the toys took on a more whimsical flavor, as did the framed movie posters on the wall. Everything was Disney, mostly *The Little Mermaid*, which made me smile. The light over his bed, which I couldn't believe I hadn't noticed the minute I walked in, was probably the only thing he'd paid more than twenty dollars for. It was a chandelier shaped like Ursula, the sea witch, each one of her eight octopus legs ending in a light bulb.

The whole thing was strange, and a little weird, and endeared him to my heart a little further.

Watson was halfway buried under the bed, his

little rump sticking in the air, his nubbin of a tail wagging at the fun of it all.

"Don't you dare chew up anything."

He didn't offer comment, which was good, as I was certain he'd be offended at the suggestion.

I gathered up the two plush dog beds, tucked one under each arm, and then I noticed two photos tucked into the corners of the framed *Lady and the Tramp* poster. With an ache in my heart, I placed Flotsam's and Jetsam's dog beds on top of Paulie's and went closer. One was of Paulie and Athena on, what I assumed, was her front porch. The other was of him, Leo, Katie, and me at Habanero's, our go-to place when we were craving Mexican food.

How sweet. How completely sweet.

Once more, tears came to my eyes. I was so glad we'd finally given him a chance. I only hated that it'd taken us so long. As I stared at the picture, I realized what was missing. These were the only photos of actual people in Paulie's life. Everything else was from movies.

I left Watson happily chuffing at whatever he'd discovered under the bed and walked through the small house once more, just to make sure I wasn't making things up.

I wasn't. There wasn't a picture to be found

anywhere. Nor, unless the furniture was family hand-me-downs, were there any heirlooms or things that looked like they'd belong to a family. Nothing. Not only was that sad, it was strange.

I debated before I took a look through his closets. Granted, the debate lasted for an entire ten seconds, but still, I debated. Within fifteen minutes or so, I was convinced that there was nothing in the house that offered any insight into Paulie's personality or his past, outside of toys and movies. But perhaps he'd had a horrible childhood. Maybe he didn't want any memories. Well... he obviously did want memories. He had the photo of the four of us together, the photo of him and Athena. So, clearly memories and people were important. Maybe he just didn't want those memories.

It had to mean something. I could feel it. And somehow be related to why he was in the hospital. Though how it could have anything to do with Melody, I couldn't imagine.

Giving up, I tapped Watson on the bottom. "Come on, buddy. Let's go home. We've got a special delivery for your new friends."

Watson just grunted and continued his exploration of the underside of Paulie's bed.

I tapped him again and got the same response.

"What in the world has you so captivated?" I got down on my hands and knees and peered underneath.

Watson's head was jammed in the opening of a large blue duffel bag. For a moment, I thought he was stuck but then noticed a gap around his neck.

Reaching in, I grabbed the strap and pulled it toward me, causing Watson to jerk his head free and back clumsily, and with great indignation, out from under the bed.

As the duffel emerged, something brown and withered rolled out as well. I couldn't tell if it had been underneath the duffel or inside it. Nor could I tell what it was before Watson snapped it between his jaws, gave one giant chew, and swallowed it whole.

I let out a cry of disgust. "Watson! What is wrong with you? We don't even know what that was? You could've just eaten beef jerky that was a hundred years old or a mummified rat."

He just grinned, then waddled off to sniff along the edges of the room, apparently satisfied.

I shuddered at the possibilities and wondered if I would be taking him to see Dr. Sallee before the night was over. The stubborn corgi wouldn't touch actual dog food, no matter how expensive the price tag—oh no, he was too good for *that*—but any piece of disgusting filth he found out in the world, he treated like filet mignon. I marveled that whatever it had been survived Flotsam and Jetsam being in the room. Though... despite Watson's snack addiction, he was a little more svelte than his compatriots. Perhaps they simply couldn't fit.

I started to shove the duffel back under the bed, and then my curiosity got the better of me. I'd already snooped through the rest of Paulie's house, might as well go for broke.

And as soon as I unzipped it the rest of the way, I knew I'd hit pay dirt.

There it was. All the things that had been missing. A bronze statue of a Scotty dog, tons and tons of papers and cards, an old Bible, and photos. More than anything, there were countless photos. Relaxing my back against the bed, I flipped through them as I sat on the floor.

Paulie hadn't changed since he was a child, it seemed, just gotten older. It was almost funny, I would've recognized him anywhere, even as an eight or nine-year-old. After a few different pictures, the people started to repeat at different ages. It was easy to guess that it was mom, dad, brother, sister, and Paulie.

There they were. Paulie's family, Paulie's past. All hidden and shoved under the bed. Why? And, more importantly, how did it tie to him lying in the hospital after being stabbed... *not* with scissors.

*Not with scissors.* In the thrill of Paulie acknowledging in his way that Athena and I were there, I'd forgotten

One more puzzle piece. And one that *almost* clicked into place. Almost....

"Fred!" At Branson's loud voice combined with the banging of the front door swinging open, I nearly jumped out of my hide. I dropped the pictures, and they fanned out over my lap, the bag, and the floor.

Watson barked, sounding more vicious than he was capable of being, and charged into the other room.

While I appreciated his gallant effort, he also left no mystery about where I was. Not that there were many options in the tiny place.

Branson's voice grew louder as he grumbled at Watson, though not unkindly, and came closer to the bedroom.

Moving quicker than I thought capable, I stuffed the pictures back into the duffel and shoved it under the bed.

I stepped on one I'd missed as I stood, snagged it quickly, and shoved it between the dog beds.

Branson stormed into the bedroom, his face furious. "We got a call from a neighbor saying a redheaded woman was breaking into Paulie's house." He folded his arms and leaned against the wall. "I'm aware you have no faith that the police know what they're doing, so you'll be surprised that it only took me one guess to figure out who it was."

Maybe it was the full night's sleep, or perhaps I'd used all the anger I had the day before. Whatever the reason, I only felt the sting of hurt at his words. Or maybe it was because I heard the sting of hurt *in* his words. "I don't think the police don't know what they're doing. Nor do I think that about you."

From the flicker of surprise on Branson's face, clearly he'd expected a battle. He relaxed ever so slightly. "Even so, I can't very well ignore you breaking and entering."

I dug in my pocket and then dangled the key between us. "No breaking, just entering. If you will recall, I'm taking care of Flotsam and Jetsam. Athena gave me the key, so I could pick up some things for them."

His green gaze flitted over the room. "You want

me to believe that's all you're doing? Just picking things up, not snooping?"

That stung too, not the accusation, but that he knew me. He really did. And yet, he was still acting this way. I snatched the stacked dog beds and held them tightly against me. Hopefully tight enough that the picture wouldn't fall out. "Yep. Just getting these and the pile of toys by the door."

"It took me a good twenty minutes to get over here, Fred." He shook his head. "Couldn't get around a herd of bighorn sheep that decided they wanted to block traffic. If that's all you were doing, you should've been gone long before I got here."

I shrugged. "I had Watson pick out which toys we should take to the dogs. He was very particular."

The corner of his lips twitched. I knew him too. He was about to laugh. It lingered, just for a second, then disappeared. "Luckily for you, Paulie's house is a pigsty, so I can't formally accuse you of going through anything. I don't see you causing the destruction in this place."

Destruction seemed a little dramatic, but I figured we didn't need to argue about anything else. Nor point out that he couldn't charge me for snooping if I'd had a key to the place.

I started to offer smart commentary about him

using the time wisely and serving me with whatever paperwork Petra had filed, if any, while we were together. But then noticed his eyes. They were sad. This wasn't like when Officer Green gave me a hard time. I could feel the enjoyment of her power play seeping off her. Branson didn't like this, maybe not much more than I did.

I took a step toward him. "Why are you doing this? I don't understand."

The hurt intensified and then disappeared behind that wall he'd become so good at erecting. Maybe he'd always been good at it. "I think the better question is, why are *you* doing this? I made it very clear what the expectations were. You're the one not obeying."

"Obeying?" I took a step back.

"Wrong word. Sorry." His cheeks flushed. "I meant—"

"No. You said what you meant." I'd already been clear on the new direction he and I were heading, but at the hurt in his eyes, I'd started to weaken. That wasn't going to happen again. "Unless you're charging me with something, I'd like to leave."

"Fred. I...." Branson stammered. He actually stammered. I wouldn't have thought it possible. But he ended with a shake of his head and twisted so I could step by him and exit the bedroom. He followed me as I hooked Watson's leash and carefully maneuvered so I could snag the four dog toys without dropping the beds.

Though I hurt somewhat as I slid into the Mini Cooper, I also had a thrill that I hadn't gotten caught taking the picture. The answer was there. I knew it.

FOUR'TEEN

"I didn't think those two actually slept." Zelda peered through the bedroom doorway at Flotsam and Jetsam from her place on my living room floor.

"Ever since I brought their beds over this afternoon, they haven't left them. I almost miss their chaos." The two had been over-the-moon ecstatic at the sight of their toys but had then crashed in their beds and not moved in hours. Every once in a while, one of them would grunt, shift, or wake slightly, but then drift back off. I wished I'd thought of getting them some of their things earlier.

"It's the music." Verona nodded sagely, also sitting on the floor, but with her back resting on the opposite end of the couch as her twin. "It soothes the soul, calms the savage beast."

Mom paused from stringing black chunky crystals into a necklace to pat Verona's shoulder. "It is lovely. I especially like the sound of the Canadian geese in the background."

"Well... this album is fine, but it's not my first choice." She cast a reproachful glare at Zelda. "The birdcalls are added in during the sound mixing. It's rather fake, and meditation music that isn't authentic can't truly cleanse the mind or soul."

Zelda remained focused on her strand of purple and pink beads. "You just watch; this series will be Chakra's top seller."

"That's exactly my point. If we choose our meditation music based on sales, then we're no different than the capitalist pigs we fight against." This time, Verona's stare was a bit more than reproachful.

Zelda was now glaring at the beads as if they'd mortally offended her. "Did it somehow miss your attention, dear sister, that we're opening a retail store?"

"That doesn't mean—"

"I have just the thing!" Mom cut off Verona with a wave of her hands and then dug in her huge tackle box of stones and crystals with a clatter. "Here we go." She withdrew two white inch-long prisms that looked like pieces of chalk with veins of gray and thrust them toward the twins. "Howlite can help rid the body of stress, pain, and... rage."

Grimacing, Zelda and Verona each took the stones and stopped their bickering. The two were nearly identical in every way. They were also similar to their father, Barry—they too wore a constant collection of tie-dye and yoga pants, though theirs were more of the natural-fiber, hand-sewn, and colored with eco-friendly dye variety than Barry's flowerchild, hippie wardrobe. For the most part, the twins shared Barry's cheerful, easygoing personality. But since starting to work on opening their new age shop together, the few differences they had seemed to be driving the other crazy. The only physical difference between them was Verona's long hair was blonde where Zelda's was brunette. For the longest time, I thought that was the only difference between them at all. Then I'd stumbled upon Zelda secretly sneaking ice cream behind her sister's back. They had a very strict no sugar and no processed food way of life. I figured it was only a matter of time before that particular difference, and a host of others came to light. When it did, I simply hoped it didn't launch World War III and take down the Cozy Corgi with it.

"I really appreciate you agreeing to move the jewelry-making party here. Flotsam and Jetsam are used to being with Paulie all the time, so I just hated to leave them again." I offered a smile at the twins over the screen of my laptop and marveled for a heartbeat that I was starting to get a grip on sister relationships. How my life had changed…. "But I am sorry I'm not helping make the jewelry myself."

Verona waved me off. "Oh, goodness, we knew you wouldn't actually make jewelry for very long."

Zelda nodded in agreement. "Even if you didn't have a murder to solve. Sometimes we wonder if Phyllis is our secret mother instead of yours. We have a lot more in common."

Like that. Comments such as that. If I didn't know the twins so well, I would've thought there was some weird competition for my mother. But there wasn't. And… they weren't exactly wrong. After all, there the three of them sat, my mother on the couch, Verona and Zelda on the floor on either side, all stringing beads and crystals together for the little space the twins were giving to my mother in their shop to sell her jewelry, while I sat across from them on the computer, with Watson snoring away at my feet.

"Well, Fred might've gotten my red hair." Mom patted her long locks, which were now silver with a streak of auburn remaining. "But she's nearly a carbon copy of her father. Which is nice. In some ways, it's like he never left." She smiled at me sweetly. "Plus, I think that's why Fred and I never went through that horrible phase during her teenage years that so many of my friends experienced with their daughters. They were too much alike, so they couldn't understand each other."

I couldn't miss the flash of longing on the twins' faces. I knew the relationship with their mother wasn't good, part of the reason they'd sought out Barry once they were adults, finding the father they'd never known. And I suppose, in my mom, also finding the mother they'd never really had.

The house fell silent for a while, comfortable with the clinking of beads, snoring and snuffling of three sleeping dogs, with the overarching sounds of flutes, chimes of meditation music, and the twittering of recorded birds. *Mostly* comfortable was more accurate, as I probably had another half an hour in me that I could handle meditation music without turning murderous, but perhaps it was doing me some good. If nothing else, it helped distract me from my hurt and anger at how Branson had been at Paulie's house while I searched endlessly on the internet for anything I could find about Paulie. I'd decided the answer lay in his past after finding the duffel. But after a couple of hours, there was nothing.

Absolutely nothing. Even on the Paws website, there was no picture of him, only Flotsam and Jetsam. It was like he didn't exist.

Which was confirmation that I was on the right track, but didn't exactly make it easier. I should've had Katie come to the crystal party. I wasn't bad at searching the internet, but she was able to work Google like it was a magic spell. However, she and Nick were spending the evening trying out new recipes for the bakery.

As the other three women in my family tinkered away with Mom's jewelry I stared at the photo I'd swiped from Paulie's home. I'd lucked out. The one that had fallen was of the entire family. The sister stood in the center, wearing a graduation cap and gown, her long brown hair caught in a breeze. She was flanked on either side by who I assumed was an older brother and Paulie. And on either side of them, the mom and dad. That had to be the story. I supposed Paulie could be a cousin or friend, but I didn't think so. They had the look of immediate family. All similar with fine, pointed features, and the way they stood indicated closeness and love.

I had the answer in my hands. I knew it, could feel it. Somehow that picture told the story. But I wasn't sure where to start. Not with Paulie unconscious and with him little more than a ghost on the internet.

The picture was nearly burned into my brain at that point, but I pored over it again, searching for some detail, some clue that I'd missed. But there was nothing. Just a normal-looking family on graduation day, with hordes of other families and various students in their matching caps and gowns in the background, a banner in the distance reading *Congratulations Class of* 2006. There weren't even any defining features. No mountains, no ocean, nothing. Although, maybe the lack of it was a defining feature. Paulie was from a place with *no* mountains. Although that was a leap. The mountains could be behind the person taking the photograph. And either way, that detail wouldn't narrow it down enough to help in the slightest. It was impossible.

"Nothing's impossible, dear. You'll figure it out."

I looked up at Mom, startled. I hadn't realized I'd spoken out loud. "I'm not so sure at the moment." I lifted the picture. "I think the answer is right here, but I just can't see it. That maybe I'm clinging to it because it's the only clue I have about Paulie. Outside of the fact that he doesn't seem to exist anywhere."

Mom stretched out her hand. "Let me see. Maybe a fresh set of eyes will help."

Readjusting the computer, I shifted so I could stretch to hand the photograph across the distance instead of standing. My foot slipped and smacked Watson on the hip.

He jumped up with a scramble of claws, huffed, gave me a glare and sauntered off toward the bedroom. He paused in the doorway, eyed the sleeping corgis, glared again, and then trundled into the kitchen.

I could practically hear him grumbling. "Sorry about that, buddy."

He didn't reply.

Mom took the picture and began to study it.

Verona was stringing a strand of white crystals together and didn't look up as she spoke. "It is strange that you can't find him anywhere. I mean, who doesn't have a Facebook profile? Even your mom's on Instagram."

"And getting quite the following, I must say." Mom shimmied happily but continued studying the photograph.

"Personally, I don't understand why you're focusing on Paulie." Zelda laid a completed piece aside and spared me a glance before scanning over other stone possibilities. "If you figure out who killed Melody, you have your answer. With Paulie being unconscious, that seems the easier route to take.

Verona rolled her eyes. "Melody's *dead*. She's not going to be any more helpful than Paulie while being unconscious."

I could see a new spat brewing, so I jumped in. "I'm actually wondering if there are two different killers... or attempted killers in Paulie's case."

All three of them paused and stared at me. It was Mom who spoke, her tone more curious than doubtful. "Really? Two at the same time? Seems like coincidence. I'm rather surprised at you. Your father never believed in coincidence. One of the areas we disagreed."

"I don't exactly believe in it either, but things just don't add up. Plus, I found out today that there were two different murder weapons. Paulie was stabbed with a knife; Melody with scissors."

Though the twins both grimaced, Mom didn't flinch.

I kept going. "It's not like I think two different people planned two separate murders and just happened to enact them at the exact same moment, but I think it does indicate that there were two people involved. Maybe teamed up, somehow. That

Paulie and Melody were connected in some way we don't know."

"Like from that picture?" Zelda took the photograph from my mom. "That girl definitely doesn't look like Melody."

"No, she doesn't. Not at all." That would've been way too easy. Unfortunately. "Plus, whereas Paulie doesn't have an online presence in the slightest, it was like the internet was invented for Melody. I can hardly find one cat website without her at least making some comment—it doesn't matter if it's a cute video or a rescue page; she was obsessed with the things. She and Jared even have a website devoted to their cats, complete with webcams. I can't understand why a person would want to, but you can sit and watch their cats sleeping in their bed." I'd kept it on in the background for several minutes, but none of the Persians had wandered by.

Zelda still studied the photograph. "Maybe someone really hates cats, and they were plotting Melody's murder, and Paulie just happened to be in the wrong place at the wrong time."

"That's ridiculous!" Verona snatched the picture from Zelda. "It happened *at* Paulie's pet shop. Someone's not going to plot to kill Melody and plan to do it there. And Paulie could hardly be in the wrong place at the wrong time at his own pet shop."

That's where I was arriving as well. "But it could work the other way around. That someone was plotting to kill Paulie, and Melody ended up being in the wrong place at the wrong time." I gestured to the photo. "Which is why it may take figuring out who was after Paulie to discover who killed Melody. She may have been an innocent bystander, but I can't find anything, not a single thing. That photo just tells me that Paulie had a family. At least I assume that's his family. But that's not exactly news. Everyone had a family, at least at one point or another."

Verona extended the photograph back to me. "It also tells you that he's from New Berlin."

I stared at her, not taking the picture back. "It tells me what?"

She shook it at me. "That he's from New Berlin. Illinois."

Mom, Zelda, and I all stared at her.

Verona tapped the picture, more specifically the T-shirt that showed through the girl's unzipped graduation gown. "That's a pretzel."

Still we stared.

She was right, there was a pretzel on the girl's T-shirt. I wasn't sure if I'd even noticed outside of it simply being the design on a T-shirt. "How does that tell you that they're from New Berlin, Illinois?"

Zelda gasped as if she understood. "Mascots!"

Verona nodded. "Obviously."

I looked back and forth between the two, but no explanation was coming. "Sorry, you're going to have to spell this one out for me. That pretzel is a mascot?"

Zelda nodded, but Verona stole the show. "Our mom married this guy named Bart Smith; he hung around for a couple years. He smelled like cheese. He was obsessed with weird sports trivia. One of his *many* charms." She shared a disgusted look with her sister. "The mascot for the high school in New Berlin, Illinois, is a pretzel."

"God, I forgot." Zelda grimaced and held the picture out to me again. "He really did smell like cheese. But more like the processed kind out of the can, you know."

I took it as if she were handing me a golden ticket and stared down as the pretzel nearly glowed from the girl's T-shirt. "You two are brilliant." Without missing another beat, I settled back into the armchair, readjusted the laptop, and did a search for the graduating class of 2006 from New Berlin, Illinois. "I can feel it. This is going to give us some answers. It may not solve the entire case but will be a step closer." I snuggled deeper into the chair, a sense of excited pleasure washing through me. "Watch me keep my nose out of this, *Sergeant* Wexler."

"Fred, don't be ungracious," Mom admonished as she pulled out a necklace from her tackle box and stood. "In fact, I made this for you after watching the interaction between you and Branson the other night at the Fourth of July." She crossed the space between us and handed me a silver chain with a green pendant. "It's an emerald. Not only your birthstone, but it is the stone for lovers. It might help you and Branson get back on track."

I'd started to take the necklace but then left it dangling from her outstretched hand. "Mom, that's sweet of you, but I have no intention of getting back on track, or anything else, with Branson."

"Now, darling, don't be hasty. Every relationship goes through rocky points. You're not going to find someone who's perfect." She kept the necklace extended toward me.

"No. I don't expect perfection, but I won't be told what to do, not in the way he's doing it especially. I don't plan on repeating mistakes."

I could see that Mom was considering her argument, and I also knew that it came from a good place.

She wanted me to be happy, wanted me to be loved. But she also couldn't fully understand. She'd had two great loves in her life, and though my father and Barry couldn't be much more different men, they were both good, loving, and kind. And both treated her like she'd hung the moon.

"I learned from my relationship with Garrett, Mom. I'm not going to repeat it."

She flinched a little and pulled the necklace back. "That's how Branson made you feel? He reminded you of Garrett?"

"Not identical, no, but enough."

She studied the emerald and then turned back to the tackle box and dropped it in. She shuffled inside, the rattling of stones and crystals filling the space as the twins and I exchanged a look. They'd heard some of the story of my life and subsequent divorce with my ex, but not all. After a few moments, Mom turned back around and held out another necklace with sky-blue crystals. "This is celestine. It helps with calming, balance, and remembering dreams. It's also perfect for Geminis, like yourself. Use this one instead."

Though I didn't put any trust in the healing properties of stones and crystals like my mother, I took it and knew I wouldn't hear one more word about her hoping I'd give Branson another chance. "Thanks, Mom."

She smiled a sweet, sad smile and then resettled on the sofa.

Maybe the calming and balancing properties of the celestine helped, or maybe it was just the twins' weird knowledge of high school mascots, but whatever it was, within five minutes I'd found the girl in the photo. Leah Bezor. Less than three minutes later, I found her Facebook page, complete with current and childhood photographs.

I joined Mom on the couch, and the twins squeezed in on either side so we could all look at the computer screen together.

"It's the same photograph." Zelda's voice was barely a whisper.

"Yeah, and his name isn't Paulie at all." Verona's tone matched.

No, it most definitely wasn't. The Bezor family was clearly labeled. Dad, Jay. Mom, Roseanne. Brother, John. Sister, Leah. And Paulie... Simon.

Hushed silence fell over us as we clicked through Leah's photographs. The most recent photo of Paulie —Simon—was only from a few years before, and he was easily recognizable. Though I wasn't sure what it meant, I was certain it had everything to do with why he was fighting for his life in the hospital.

Zelda chuckled suddenly. "The whole family kind of look like mice. The way their chins and noses are so pointy. Even their teeth. All they really need are whiskers."

Verona reached across Mom and me to smack her twin. "That's a horrible thing to say. True, they're not the most attractive family in the world, but they hardly deserve to be compared to rodents."

Zelda gasped and clutched her arm. "And I don't deserve to be hit. That wasn't an insult. Mice are adorable. Not as cute as chipmunks, but still."

At their words, I let out a gasp of my own and tapped Leah Bezor's face on the screen as realization dawned. She was now around thirty, and Zelda was right, Leah did have a rather mousy appearance. She'd also bleached her long hair. "This is Paulie's mystery woman. He wasn't having an affair. He was secretly meeting with his sister."

After another full night's sleep, followed by a walk at the crack of dawn with my pack of puppies, Watson and I arrived at the Cozy Corgi half an hour before opening time. Typically, I would've curled up in the mystery room and taken the opportunity to get lost in a book. Instead, I went to the bakery for breakfast dessert and a dirty chai.

Katie and Nick were already there, deep into another round of baking. Just watching them made me want to go back to bed. "I definitely chose the right career path when I fell in love with books. If they ever demand I get up at ungodly hours of the morning, it's just because I'm so intrigued with a novel that I need to know what happens; they don't require me to toil away over an oven."

"Are you kidding? Coming in here every morning has been the best part of my life!" Nick grinned happily over at me, nearly covered to his elbows with flour. "But you sound like Ben. He's either reading a book or writing a story at all times."

Katie nodded along. "I have to admit, since Nick came on board, I'm enjoying things quite a bit more myself. The long hours aren't quite so strenuous when you've got a baking buddy." She winked at him affectionately and then refocused on me. "We lucked out with these two. We really did. But things will ease up eventually. We won't be selling out every single day forever. Tourist season will end, and at some point, Carla will reopen the Black Bear Roaster."

Carla owned one of the popular coffee shops in town, and she'd closed it a couple of months ago over a scandal. Katie kept referencing her reopening. I wasn't so certain she would. But I hoped so.

Nick made an unusually sour face but offered no comment. He'd worked for Carla and hadn't had the best of experiences, but it wasn't in his nature to speak ill of anyone or speak much at all, for that matter. Both brothers were quiet, but Nick was the more reserved of the twins. It was the only way to tell them apart, that and the scar on Nick's eyebrow compared to the scar on Ben's lip. Oh, and Watson's hero-worship of Ben.

Katie slid a tray of cinnamon rolls into the oven and then dusted her hands. "So, who's on your list today, Fred? Since you think you found Paulie's sister, are you going to take her picture to Delilah, see if she's the same woman Delilah saw with Paulie?"

"That's not a bad idea, actually." I'd been about to take a bite of my apple fritter but paused to respond. Beside me, Watson whimpered. I tossed a morsel to him, and he trotted away happily. "I texted it to Athena this morning, as I was afraid it was too late last night, but I haven't heard back. Really though, it's the only thing that makes sense. I'm sure it's her."

"It's so weird to think that Paulie isn't actually Paulie. That he's some guy named Simon."

Nick nodded along with Katie's sentiment.

"Are you kidding?" I couldn't help but laugh. "*You* find it weird that someone is living a double life with a secret past?"

Katie shrugged. "*I* wasn't living a double life. I just had a secret past. It's not the same thing." She shrugged again. "At least... not exactly."

From the corner of my eye, I saw Watson trotting my way again, and I popped the remaining too-large bite into my mouth. I kept my gaze focused on Nick and Katie, so I wouldn't have to feel his judgment.

Katie changed the subject as my mouth was full. "I was looking into Melody's website that you told me about—that thing is intense. Did you read her blogs?"

I shook my head, still not done chewing.

"She blogged about those cats every day. About each one of them." She widened her eyes. "From their perspective. Each cat had their own diary. She'd even started one for Belvedere and Cameo, and they hadn't even arrived yet."

"Wow." Nick gave a shake of his head in wonder as he sliced a loaf of chocolate dough into biscotti shapes. "That's even more intense than my brother, and I didn't think anyone liked animals as much as Ben."

Katie scrunched her nose. "I don't know. If Jared is as allergic as we've heard, I'd say he might love them more than Melody. Why else would he put himself through such torture?"

Now finally free to speak—I should have just given another bite to Watson after all—I was able to chime in. "I kinda feel like he did it because he loved Melody so much, not the cats."

Katie shook her head. "No. I thought so at first, but I think he had to love them as much as she did. The morning of her death, Melody blogged all about it. It was her and Jared's tenth wedding anniversary. She bought that cat castle for Jared." She snorted out a laugh. "Well, not for Jared, I don't think he was going to crawl in it or anything, but as a surprise for their cats. If that's what she got him for their anniversary, they must mean as much to him as they did to her."

"I don't think so." At his disagreement, Nick's voice was even quieter than normal. Katie and I both focused on him, causing him to blush. "Now that Ben and I have our own place, he wanted to get a pet. A dog, but since we're only in an apartment, he's settling for a cat. We went to the animal rescue last night. All of the cats were there."

"You mean all of *Jared and Melody's* cats were there? As in all seven of the *Persian* cats were at the shelter?" I couldn't believe my ears. "You think Jared put the cats up for adoption?"

He nodded. "Yeah. We adopted Cinnamon."

Katie and I exchanged glances, and I had to reevaluate how I'd thought of Jared. That would explain why I hadn't seen any cats on the live web feed the night before. "Maybe he doesn't love her like I thought he did. Dumping all the cats that she was obsessed with at a pound? Where they might get euthanized?"

"Oh no." Nick shook his head hurriedly. "They don't do that there. It's a really good facility. I guarantee you, they'll all get a home. They're in a *very* good place."

"But still...." Katie sounded dumbstruck. "Even if that's true, I can't imagine Jared putting them in a place where they'd be split up. Surely he would know that would displease Melody."

"Katie, who in their right mind is going to adopt seven cats?" The thought nearly made me shudder.

"Okay, fair point." She narrowed her eyes at me before she sucked in a little gasp. "Fred, you don't think... I mean, I get that he's allergic, but that's really quick. They haven't even had Melody's funeral yet."

"You're right. That is really fast." The memory of Jared's reaction when he found Melody played through my mind. It simply didn't feel right for him to be getting rid of his beloved wife's cats so quickly after she was killed.

"You think Jared killed his wife?" Nick caught on just a few seconds later. "And tried to hurt Paulie?"

The three of us stared at one another.

Maybe that was what I was implying.

Before I could think of what to say, there was a

knock below on the door, causing all three of us to jump and Watson to give a sharp bark.

I glanced at the time; we were five minutes late opening. "Okay, let's not jump to conclusions. Let's just think about this. I'll glance through the blog during a break in customers and see if I can read between the lines on any of Melody's posts. In the meantime, I'll go check with Delilah about Paulie's sister. Maybe swing by the animal rescue and see if I can talk to anyone who was there when Jared dropped off the cats."

It was a couple of hours before Ben came in and there was enough of a lull in the tourists that I could sneak away to talk to Delilah. I snapped the leash on Watson's collar as we walked out the front door. "All right, little man, let's go visit your new favorite person."

As we crossed the street, I angled toward Madame Delilah's Old Tyme Photography.

"Fred!"

I'd nearly reached the other side and looked toward the voice. Carl Hanson waved frantically out of the front door of Cabin and Hearth. Adjusting, we headed his way.

He grinned and continued waving, sweat glistening off his bald head and causing his glasses to slide down his chubby cheeks. "We saw you coming over, but we thought you were headed our way." Despite his smile, he sounded offended.

"No, I was actually going to see Delilah."

His eyes went wide. "Really? Do you think she killed Melody?"

"Carl!" I glanced around us at the tourists, seeing if any of them overheard. "What a thing to say." I hated to think what Delilah would do if she heard that rumor.

Although... she'd probably like the attention.

"Well, we've been wondering...." He let his words trail away and gave an exaggerated shrug.

Carl and his wife were the royalty of gossip in Estes Park, so their wondering about Delilah Johnson being a murderer hardly served as an indictment. Chances were they'd tossed around every name in town as a possibility. But the pair was a good source of information, and I'd grown truly fond of them. Might as well see if they had any tidbits that might point away from Jared. I just couldn't see him doing it, but I was aware that could be because I simply didn't want to believe it. "Are you busy right now?"

He shook his head and opened the door wide for

Watson and me to pass. "No, not at all. In fact—" He flicked the lock and flipped the Closed sign. "—we're all yours."

As we walked toward the counter, Anna gave me an unusually cold stare. "Too good to talk to us now, Fred? I thought you always came to us first when you were investigating a murder."

I was surprised, she actually looked like her feelings were hurt. "Anna, you know I'm not actually investigating—" Her stare grew impossibly icier and made me change directions. "I've actually really been off the past couple of days. I can't even explain why. Be glad I haven't come by till now."

Carl, moving slower than me, caught up at the counter. "Well, I have to admit, it does sound that way. Petra was livid the other night at the Feathered Friends Brigade about you accusing her."

"Oh, Petra!" Anna waved him off. "She's always upset about something or other." She refocused on me, her eyes a little less frigid. "Well, you're here now. And..." She leaned over the counter, and every last bit of ice melted away. "You brought my favorite soul in the whole world."

Watson beamed up at her, knowing exactly what was coming.

"Carl!" Anna swatted her husband. "Go get Watson one of those dog treats he loves so much."

He gaped at her and pointed at me. "I just got Fred when you—"

She cut him off with another icy glare, and after two seconds, Carl puffed away toward the back.

"Anna, you don't have to do that. Katie makes them all the time for him now."

She looked scandalized. "Where do you think I get them? And of course I have to. He loves them." She pointed at Watson. "Just look at him, so excited for his little treat."

Sure enough, with the repeat of his favorite word, Watson gave a double bounce on his front paws. He sure knew how to work it, I'd give him that.

By the time Carl rejoined us, Anna had left her spot behind the counter and was lavishing affection on Watson. As always, he did little more than grin and bear it, knowing where the exuberant petting would lead.

Anna snatched the dog bone biscuit from Carl and held it to Watson like an offering. "Here you go, my little love muffin."

Watson snatched the treat, and as always, turned and hurriedly waddled away, this time taking shelter under a large ottoman with legs made from elk antlers.

Anna watched him in satisfaction for several moments and then turned to me, excitement in her voice. "So, I overheard you tell Carl that you think Delilah did it. I'm not surprised; a hussy like that's capable of anything."

It took all my effort not to sigh. "I didn't say that. I don't think Delilah had anything to do with it."

Both of their expressions fell simultaneously.

"You don't?" Carl pushed his glasses up again. "She could be... what do you call it?" He snapped his fingers. "A man-eater! Maybe she was after Jared, so she took out the competition. Although why a beautiful woman like her would need to resort to murder to—" His eyes went wide as Anna whipped toward him at that declaration, and he smartly took a step back, out of arm's reach.

Pausing to let her glare linger, Anna finally cleared her throat and returned to me. "You're right, of course. That makes no sense at all. I'm sure Delilah didn't kill Melody, and even if she did, that wouldn't make any sense as to why she would try to kill Paulie. *He* wasn't married to Jared."

"Oh... right." Carl sounded disappointed. "I didn't think about that."

I nearly brought up the theory that two different people had killed Melody and tried to kill Paulie, but decided against it. Not to mention, I couldn't quite make that scenario play out in my head; it made no sense. Talk about coincidences. It didn't add up. Plus, as much as I hated to think of it, if Jared was responsible, perhaps he did blame Paulie for aiding his wife's cat obsession. Though, that still didn't explain why he used scissors on his wife and a knife on Paulie.

Anna tapped her round nose and pointed at me. "You have a theory. I can tell. Who do you think?"

Carl shuffled closer.

I debated once more, but that time I opted to go for it. "Though I can't see him doing it, I'm wondering about Jared. With as—"

I couldn't finish mentioning his allergies before they both shook their heads emphatically, and Anna cut me off. "No. Absolutely not. He wouldn't do that. That man loved his wife."

"I thought so too, but there are too many—"

Again Anna jumped in and was so passionate that for second, I thought I was going to be on the receiving end of one of her slaps. "He wouldn't. Why, right before Melody was killed, he came in here. She'd *just* given him their anniversary present."

Carl nodded along.

"Their anniversary present?" I had to make sure I wasn't mishearing. "The cat castle from Paws?"

They both nodded, but it was Carl who answered. "Yeah. Melody surprised him. Put a big bow on it and everything. Jared was on his way to get their car so they could take it home."

Something wasn't adding up. "Why did Jared come in here?"

Anna angled her head toward Carl. "We saw him walking by, wanted to ask him about Pete Miller. There was a little tidbit Carl overheard while he was at the bird club but couldn't ask about it then, obviously."

I could see that happening easily enough. They'd just done something similar to me, after all.

Carl shot a reproachful look at Anna. "We weren't only trying to get gossip. Jared is our friend. We don't use our friends for gossip."

"No, of course we don't," Anna agreed whole-heartedly, then refocused on me. "It started to rain while he was in here, so he waited out the storm until it was a little slower and he could go get his vehicle. Providence, if you ask me. He simply needed to talk. The poor man...." Anna paused and leaned back to the counter to dig through a pile of papers, then withdrew the announcement of Belvedere and Cameo. "Melody put these in the mail to go out to all the store owners in advance but surprised Jared with the news that morning as well, right before they drove into town so she could surprise him with the castle. Another anniversary gift." She clucked her tongue. "You should have seen him. I swear he was near tears. Poor man didn't want any more cats. But even then... even in the midst of worrying about having nine cats and how many more shots he'd have to take, he was making us promise we'd never repeat what he was saying. That he didn't want it to get back to Melody and hurt her feelings. She didn't know how miserable he was, the poor lamb."

I gaped at her, shocked that she didn't realize what she was saying, that she was spelling out the very motive I'd been considering.

Suddenly she looked concerned. "I don't think we're breaking that confidence now, do you? I mean, she's *dead*. It can't hurt her feelings any longer."

Before I could think of a reply, my phone rang. Checking it, I saw Athena's name on the display. I held up a finger toward Anna and Carl. "I'm so sorry, I need to get this very quickly."

Maybe she was calling back to confirm that Leah Bezor was the woman she'd seen Paulie with.

I'd forgotten Paulie's secret family amid what I was learning about Jared. How in the world could the two things be connected?

I lifted the phone to my ear. "Athena, hi. I take it you got my photo? Is she—"

"Fred!" Athena's voice was excited, not at all like her normally reserved and classy tone. "He's awake! Paulie is awake!"

SIXTEEN

Paulie offered a wince of a smile as Watson and I rushed into the hospital room. "Fred." His voice was weak and scratchy, but it was there. That was all that mattered. He was alive and awake and at least cognizant enough to recognize me. All good signs.

Athena sat beside him, her hand in his, Pearl peeking over the edge of her purse from Athena's lap. She let out an excited yip at the site of Watson.

Giving a little hop of happiness, Watson started to trot to her, then paused as he bristled and looked across the room.

I'd been about to greet Paulie but glanced at what had caught Watson's attention.

Branson stood in the corner, next to another large man in uniform. He looked familiar, but I couldn't place his name.

For a second, I stood frozen, irrationally thinking

I'd stumbled into a setup of some sort, then pushed that aside. I hadn't done anything illegal, and much more importantly, Paulie was awake. Turning back, I finished the short distance to Paulie's side and took his other hand. "Hey there. It's so good to see you. Glad you're back with us."

Another grin. "Me too."

Athena released Paulie's hand, snatched a cup off the table, and held out a small spoon of ice chips to Paulie's lips. "Here, you sound horrible."

He took the ice and winced once more.

"Remember, don't chew or swallow it. Just let it melt, like the nurse told you." Athena smoothed her fingers through Paulie's hair in a motherly fashion. Then she looked at me. "The doctors are saying it's a miracle. Of course, they'll have to do more tests, but from the way he is, it seems like Paulie is going to make a full recovery." She smiled down at him and gave another loving stroke to his thinning hair.

Paulie winked. "All that means is that I know everybody's names and that I unfortunately still remember who's president."

"Yeah, sounds like you really will make a full recovery." Tears of relief stung my eyes as I laughed. "Your boys miss you. I'll make sure to tell them when I get home tonight."

"They were the first things he asked about." Athena kept her attention on Paulie. "Just like any good doggy daddy should."

"Thanks for watching them, Fred." Paulie's voice sounded a little better, but so tired. "I know they're a handful."

"That they are. But... I think they've stolen our hearts. Even Watson's." That might've been a touch of an exaggeration, but he tolerated them more than before, so I figured that was close enough.

"Speaking of dogs, it strikes me that we might need to check the laws that are on the books about canines in public facilities."

The three of us looked over at the gruff voice from the corner.

The man scowled at Watson. "This might be a small tourist trap of a town, but we're not a bunch of backward hillbillies. We don't need flea-ridden animals in a hospital."

Athena bristled, sitting straighter, and shot daggers at him. "The only one of us in here that's flea-ridden is—"

"Fred, I don't know if you two have met." Branson cut her off, but the action seemed almost protective as opposed to rude. He gestured toward the man. "This is Police Chief Rusty Briggs." He then gestured at me. "This is Winifred Page. She—"

"Trust me, Wexler, everyone knows who *this* is." His gaze traveled over me, something bordering between dismissal and repulsion. "You like to play policewoman, instead of keeping your nose in your books."

The emotions flipping from relief and gratefulness at Paulie's recovery to the horrible mix of anger and unjustifiable embarrassment left me speechless.

"I've read about your father, Ms. Page." Though Chief Briggs's voice had suddenly lost its sarcastic tone, his eyes grew colder. "He died a hero's death in the line of duty."

I searched for a response; typically, such a comment would endear a person to me, but I could feel the cut coming before the blade emerged.

"Can't help but think he'd be ashamed at the way his daughter disrespects the badge."

Proving once more that he understood more words than I realized, or simply could read a person's intentions, a low rumble issued from Watson's chest.

The police chief didn't bother looking down, keeping his gaze on me. "I *do* know we have laws on the books about aggressive animals being kept as pets."

"I can attest that Watson is not an aggressive animal, sir." To my surprise, Branson put a hand on his superior's shoulder and stepped forward. "Paulie, do you want to explain things to Fred or would you like me to?"

Despite it being obvious that Branson was clearly attempting to rescue me by changing the subject, I could've sworn I felt a chill pass between him and Paulie. Although with Paulie being in pain and me being tempted to launch myself across the room to tear the police chief to shreds, I didn't trust my perceptions to be on target.

Paulie took a second, swallowed, winced, and then managed to croak, "Go ahead."

Athena provided him with another small mound of ice.

Chief Briggs shook off Branson's hand. "Sergeant Wexler, Ms. Page isn't entitled to any explanation."

"Yes, she is." Paulie glared at the police chief for a moment, and then his gaze flicked to me. "Athena says you already figured out some of it, not that I'm surprised." He grinned slightly and looked back at Branson. "Tell her."

Branson hesitated, clearly waiting to see if the chief was going to stop the conversation. He didn't. It was bizarre seeing Branson in a subservient role. Finally, he looked at me and began. "Paulie, as you already know, it seems, is Simon Bezor. He's in the witness protection program. Or... was. It was of the utmost importance for his safety that his secret remained intact. No one could know. Not even his friends." Though his words were matter-of-fact, the plea for understanding was clear in his eyes.

From Athena's shocked stare, it was clear she hadn't known either.

Witness protection program. It sounded too far-fetched to be real. I studied Paulie—Simon. He'd always seemed so nervous and jumpy. I'd thought it was simply his personality, but maybe it hadn't been. Perhaps he'd just truly been afraid. "Why? Do you mind if I know?"

Paulie shook his head.

"That's none of your business. Ms. Pa—"

"Paulie worked in a toy factory in Illinois." Though Branson cut off his superior, he kept his gaze focused on me. Again, it felt like he was attempting to make amends. "He discovered that it was a cover for trafficking drugs and illegal firearms. Thanks to him, the feds carried out a successful sting and raided the facility. They arrested all those involved, except for Charles Franklin, who was the kingpin of the entire operation. He slipped through their fingers."

"Charles Franklin?" At the name, my blood ran cold, and I plopped into the chair beside Paulie's bed. Watson hurried over from where he'd been curled up with Pearl.

Paulie looked at me in concern. "You know that name?"

"Yeah." I nodded at Paulie and then looked back at Branson. "He was involved in the case that my dad was working on when he was killed. He wasn't arrested at the time, but he was believed to be more on the periphery of it all, too."

"He moved up the ranks, it seems, or the ones doing the investigation into your dad's death didn't have all the information." Genuine sympathy crossed Branson's face. "Are you okay? I don't have to keep going if this is too much."

It did feel like too much. The last thing I'd expected was anything connected to my father. But the world could've stopped and I would've demanded Branson keep going. "No, I want it all."

"Like I was saying, he was the only one who got away from that raid, and, as things go, the one they needed most. Not one of the others involved in the ring was willing to accept a plea bargain to turn on

Charles Franklin. Not one, which lets you know how dangerous the man is. As a result, Paulie is the one witness we have linking Mr. Franklin to his crimes. The only choice the authorities felt they had was to put Paulie in protective custody and into the witness protection program. When he was relocated here, Chief Briggs and myself were the only two given his true identity. Things have stayed safe for him ever since." He shot a glare at Paulie. "Until recently."

It only took a moment for me to guess what caused the tension between Branson and Simon. Although it seemed everyone was still going to refer to him as Paulie, which worked well for me. I looked at him. "Your sister. Leah."

"Yeah. My sister. You really are good, Fred." He smiled, a sad, sweet thing. "She showed up a couple of weeks ago. Found the Paws website and took a guess that it was me when she saw Flotsam and Jetsam on the main page. I always had a thing for corgis, and she said she knew the minute she saw their names that it was me."

"Paulie refused to quit seeing her and also refused to relocate." Branson joined in again. "That would've been protocol. When a person's identity is revealed, they're supposed to start over—new place, new name, do it all over again."

Paulie reached for my hand so he was grasping both Athena and me. "I wasn't going to leave my new life. My friends." He smiled. "I miss my family, desperately, but even back in my old life, my real one, I never had such good friends."

"And it nearly killed you." Chief Briggs's dislike of Paulie was evident in his venom-laced words. "And your selfishness cost an innocent woman her life."

"There's no call for that." Athena turned her fury on the police chief. "Paulie is not responsible for someone else taking a life. He didn't—"

"No. He's right." Paulie sounded defeated, completely guilt-ridden. "If I had listened, if I had left, Melody wouldn't have died." Emotion mixed with the scratchiness of his voice. I realized that for him, Melody's death was brand-new.

Though Athena shook her head, the room fell silent.

Finally, at long last, the puzzle pieces were clicking into place. All the secrets, the confusion. Even Branson's abrupt turn of face. He'd been doing his job. He wouldn't have been able to tell me about Paulie's real identity.

But *Charles Franklin*. I couldn't believe it. After all these years. His name showing up here in Estes

Park. I heard Mom's voice in the back of my head, reminding me that my father didn't believe in coincidences.

"Paulie... er... Simon?"

He grinned at me. "You can call me Paulie."

"Okay." That was easier and less strange on my tongue. "Was it Charles Franklin that hurt you, who killed Melody? You saw him?"

I expected Briggs to interrupt, but either he'd given up or Paulie spoke too quickly. "I did see him. Yes. It was Charles."

Again ice ran through my veins. One of the men involved in my father's death had been across the street from me. He had been in the same town as my mother and myself. Maybe still was. "What happened?"

"It's all still kind of a blur." His voice cracked, and Athena gave him more ice chips.

Maybe I was being selfish, pushing too hard. "You just woke up. You don't have to go into all of this."

Athena nodded. "She's right, Paulie. It can wait. The doctors didn't even want us to be in here, let alone putting you through the trauma again."

"No. I want to." He smiled at Athena, took a second to glare at Branson and Briggs across the room, then looked at me. "The day was crazy. Leah came by that morning. I was pretty sure Delilah Johnson saw me letting her in the back door from the alley. While Leah was there, I got a phone call. I thought it was Melody saying they were on their way, so I answered. It was Petra. She'd just gotten Melody's announcement about the two new cats, and she was furious. Worried that with even more cats, there was a greater chance of them getting in and killing her birds again." Paulie chuckled. "I figured she was going to have that reaction, not that I blamed her. I was prepared. I'd ordered a new extra-strength cat repellent that she could spray around her house. It had just come in the day before. That seemed to satisfy her." He laughed again. "I can't even blame her for being concerned. She was already having trouble with the Pitts having seven cats, and now there was going to be more. I'd tried to talk Melody out of getting Belvedere and Cameo, but she was determined. I love animals, but I can't imagine having nine cats. I can't even imagine having nine corgis."

Petra. My skin tingled at her name. "Petra was there?"

"No. She didn't have time to come down right then. They were slammed at the ice cream shop. I never got the chance to give Petra the cat repellent." He sighed. "Not that it matters now, I suppose."

"So, Petra *wasn't* there?"

"Good Lord!" Chief Briggs slapped his thigh in frustration, causing both dogs to bark, which only made him glower more. "Are you daft, woman? He just said the ice cream lady was too busy to come by."

I didn't spare him a glance, just offered an encouraging smile to Paulie. "Keep going. What do you recall?"

"It was during that big downpour, remember?"

I nodded.

"Melody and Jared came in right before the rain. She bought that cat castle, you know." He didn't wait for me to respond before he continued. "It was their anniversary, and she surprised him." His brows knitted slightly. "He was, surprised, that is. But I don't think he was overly happy about it, but Melody didn't seem to notice. Jared went to get the car. He and I were going to dismantle the castle and load it up for them to take home. Then it started to rain, *really* rain. While we waited, Melody went to the restroom. She wasn't feeling very well. I went back to the storeroom to get the tools to tear down the castle. I heard a noise and thought it was Leah. I turned around to find Charles there. Before I could do anything, he stabbed me." Paulie closed his eyes, wincing at the memory. "He pulled the knife out and was going to do it again, but I managed to knock it out of his hand." He gave a horrible laugh. "For all the good it did. He grabbed something off the shelf and bashed me on the head. I don't even know what it was, just that it was heavy and it hurt. I don't remember the rest."

"We found Charles last night. He was hiding out in a cave in Glen Haven." Branson brought my attention back to him. "We... weren't able to bring him in alive. It's over. Paulie is safe."

Paulie sighed at that. "And Melody is avenged. I'll never stop feeling responsible, but maybe that will help Jared."

"That is not your fault, Paulie." Athena's tone left no room for argument. "It isn't."

Something still wasn't sitting correctly. "Hold on... Charles stabbed Paulie with a knife, which Paulie got away from him, and then he hits Paulie in the head with something." I met Branson's gaze and made clear that I wasn't just going to smile and go along with the story. "And then what? He goes out into the pet shop and stabs Melody with scissors? So we now have one killer who used *three* different weapons?"

"Here we go. Apparently, your reputation isn't unwarranted." Chief Briggs rolled his eyes.

I didn't even glance his way, just kept focused on Branson. "There was no one else in the pet shop when I went in. I didn't hear anything outside of the dogs and the other animals being upset. No one running away. No one tried to hurt me. I didn't interrupt the scene. And if I did, why wouldn't Charles have gone after me? He'd already killed Melody. If his whole purpose in all of this was to kill Paulie to keep him from testifying, he didn't do a very good job."

Branson cocked his head, and I could see the realization in his eyes. And the agreement.

"You think someone else was there?" Athena sounded intrigued more than skeptical. "That someone else killed Melody?"

"This is ridiculous." Chief Briggs turned to Branson with an incredulous expression. "You're *dating* this woman? How do you maintain your sanity?"

Branson said something, and I thought he came to my defense, but I didn't listen. Nor did I care. I replayed Paulie's story in my mind as they bickered, matching it up with my experience when I'd walked in on the scene. The stillness of the pet shop, save for the panic of the animals. The bow on the castle. The large tag with Jared's name. The crumpled-up announcement of Belvedere and Cameo on the floor. Melody's body halfway behind the counter.

At long last, all the puzzle pieces clicked. At least I was fairly certain they did.

By the time the nurse came in, demanding that Paulie have some rest, I had a plan in place. I just wasn't sure if I could pull it off. Even if I could, it wasn't one hundred percent guaranteed to work.

SEVENTEEN

In a town the size of Estes Park, news traveled quicker than the speed of light. A part of my plan required the element of surprise and shock. Actually, I wasn't certain if it was required, but it would help. Even if that part succeeded, I still wasn't certain it would work. Either way, the events fell into place in record time.

I waited in Paulie's room until Branson and the police chief left. Branson attempted to talk to me alone, but I claimed I didn't want to leave Paulie's side. Once they were gone, I shared my suspicions with Athena and Paulie, got his permission, and then enlisted Athena, Katie, and Leo to help me enact my scheme.

From my position in the empty hospital room next to

Paulie, I watched through the narrow window of the door as Petra walked past. I counted to five, then opened the door wide enough for Watson to exit and for me to slip through with my arms full, then paused outside the doorway to Paulie's room, just within earshot.

"Paulie, I'm so sorry." Though I couldn't see her face, Petra sounded sincere. Enough that it made me wonder if I was making a mistake. "I was so relieved when Athena called and said you were awake."

"Thanks for coming. She told you I don't have much time left?" Paulie's voice was raspier than when he'd first woken up. I wasn't sure if he was doing it for effect or if he was simply wearing out.

"She did. But surely the doctors are wrong. Don't give up hope. Wherever there is life, there's still hope." There was the squeak of a chair, which I assumed was Petra sitting down beside Paulie's bed.

"No." Paulie's tone was resigned, yet mournful. "The doctor says that things might've been different if I'd gotten help earlier but that the damage is irreversible now. That I'd lain there too long without assistance."

As I listened to Paulie deliver his lines, I feared I'd made a mistake. Though I had no medical training, that logic sounded preposterous. If it had been true, Paulie would hardly be doing well enough to talk to her about it.

Several moments passed before Petra responded. "I wish things would've been different, Paulie." I thought I detected wariness in her tone.

Second-guessing my original plan, I reached out and knocked on the door of the room I'd just exited and then stepped into Paulie's ahead of schedule.

Paulie's eyes widened in surprise as I rounded the corner, and Petra turned to face us at the sound of Watson's nails clattering on the linoleum.

She flinched at the sight of us and paled slightly as she noticed the huge cinnamon-colored Persian cat in my arms.

"Hi, Petra." I leveled my gaze and walked to the other side of the bed, then placed Cinnamon on Paulie's lap. "Nice of you to come see Paulie while you still can."

"Isn't that...?" She looked back and forth between me, Paulie, and the cat, then shook her head, clearly deciding it couldn't be the cat she thought it was. She looked like she was about to say something else and then stood, looking toward the door.

"Wait." Paulie never stopped stroking Cinnamon.

Petra simply shook her head again and started to walk back across the room.

"Don't leave yet. You already walked away from me once."

Petra flinched and whipped back toward Paulie. "Excuse me?"

"You heard me." Some of the exhaustion left his tone. "You already left me when I was dying once."

She was white as a ghost and nearly as quiet. "I don't know what you're talking about." She headed for the door.

Before Petra made it more than a couple of feet, Leo walked in, holding Finnegan. It seemed the gray cat felt similarly toward Leo as Watson, as he kept licking Leo's face. Leo didn't speak, but came to a stop an arm's length away from Petra, standing between her and the door.

A muffled sneeze reverberated from another room.

Petra looked frantically between the two Persians. This time, it was clear she knew exactly who these cats were.

Before she could do anything else, Pete Miller entered holding the black shaggy Leroy. Pete stopped beside Leo.

Petra took a step back, looking as if she were

considering getting a running start and booking it around them toward the door. She looked even tinier than ever. "What are you doing?"

No one replied, and a few seconds later, Carl entered, holding the blonde Sherbet, quickly followed by Anna—who'd refused to be left out—walking in followed by the snow-white Ethel on a pink leash.

Petra swallowed and cleared her throat. "What is this?" She sounded panicked and a bit afraid.

"Just members of your family, the bird club, here to be with Paulie." Myrtle entered, Beatrice, another black Persian draped over her arms. "We take care of our own, remember?" Myrtle had looked judgmental and harsh many times, but I'd never seen her appear quite so fierce as she took her spot beside Anna. "Or did you forget that part of belonging to the Feathered Friends Brigade when you ran away while Paulie was dying?"

"I... I...." Petra staggered back another step or two and then seemed to come to her senses, or at least found her temper. "I have no idea what you're talking about. I never ran away from Paulie. I would never do that. And I resent—"

A loud sneeze cut her off, and Jared, red and puffy-eyed, walked in, cradling a calico-colored

Angel in his arms, his eyes blazing at Petra. The two of them stared at each other in silence for several heartbeats.

Until that moment, I hadn't been sure. Not completely. I thought I knew, but there'd still been the tiniest flicker of doubt.

Either way, I was certain Melody's killer was going to be in the room by the time the last person entered.

I was relieved to see that my gut had been right.

"How could you?" Jared sneezed again, handed Angel to Myrtle and took a step toward Petra. "Melody was the best person in the world. How could you hurt her?"

"How dare—" Petra caught herself, shook her head sharply, and readjusted her tone to one of sympathy. "I don't blame you, Jared. You're going through a rough time." She flicked an angry gaze my way but remained in control as she focused on Jared again. "You've been listening to *her*. It makes sense that you'd want to find someone to blame, but she doesn't know what she's talking about."

"You're a liar." Jared's clenched fists trembled as he raised them and he took another step forward.

I moved between them, both to keep Jared from doing something that would get him into trouble and to push the envelope one final step. I thrust the recently crumpled pink announcement of Belvedere and Cameo's arrival at Petra. "You left this behind."

She caught it on instinct and paled further. If there'd been even an ounce of doubt remaining, it died at the look on her face.

Watson and I both moved closer. I opted to push, and push hard. I couldn't give her a chance to think through it, no second to calm down. "It was the final straw, wasn't it, Petra? Melody's cats had already killed one of your birds, and now she was adding two more. I can't even say I blame you. What normal person would have seven cats, let alone nine?"

Her eyes twitched in agitation. Though it could've easily been directed at me, I was willing to bet it was at the memory of Melody and her cats.

"You didn't mean to do it, did you?" I kept going. "You went to Paws to get the cat repellent from Paulie. You were just going to protect your birds."

Petra glanced toward Paulie, then back at me.

Time to go in for the kill. "You never dreamed Melody would be there. You lost control. You didn't plan it, didn't even mean it. You just saw her, grabbed the closest thing handy, and did what you needed to do to protect—" I tried to remember the names and couldn't. "—your parrots."

Her mouth fell open, and it looked like Petra was about to concede, but then she shook her head. "No. You're crazy."

I was losing her. I felt the moment like it was slipping through my fingers. I was losing her, and I couldn't think of a way to jab the knife in one more time.

"I can't blame you for protecting Ra and Horus." Myrtle stepped around me, sounding understanding at first, but then she thrust an open hand toward Paulie, and all compassion vanished. "But how could you leave *him*? How could you leave Paulie? He's one of ours. He's part of our family."

"I wasn't going to!" The words burst from Petra in a defiant scream, and then her voice lowered, angry and cold. "I went in, hollered for Paulie, heard a noise in the back and went to him. He was lying there, bleeding to death. I thought he might already be dead." She looked at him. "You looked dead; you really did. Even if you weren't, there was so much blood.... I didn't think there would be any way to save you. But I tried." She faltered then. "At least... I was going to. I hurried back out to use your phone to call for help, and then...." She shook her head. "And then...."

"You saw my wife." Tears streamed down Jared's

checks, from red eyes so swollen from the cats that it seemed impossible he could see. "You ran out of that room and found Melody. And you killed her."

"You should be thanking me, you idiot." Petra whirled on Jared, pure hatred covering her face. "What kind of man are you?" A sneer cut her lips. "Look at you now. You can barely breathe. Don't act like you're not relieved. Some part of you knows I did you a favor. You were desperate to be free." She made a sweeping gesture, encompassing the cats. "You got rid of those horrid monsters before Melody's body was even cold."

"You evil—" Jared started to lunge, but Leo grabbed his shoulder, holding him in place.

Petra nearly fell backward in her effort to avoid Jared but caught herself. In that moment, a fresh look of horror washed over her face, clearly realizing all that she'd said. She turned her hate-filled eyes on me. Her mouth moved as if she was getting ready to curse, and then she shut it and darted past.

Just as we'd discussed when we went over the plan and what might happen, the members of the bird club parted and let her rush out.

Watson darted after her.

"No!" I slapped my thigh. "Watson. Come here."

He halted, skidding over the linoleum at his

speed, not managing to stop until he was out the door. He glared back at me, confused.

"Good boy." I patted my thigh again. "Come here, good boy."

He looked longingly at Petra's retreating form down the hall and then sauntered back in to plop down at my feet, looking utterly thwarted.

I ruffled his ears. "It's okay. She won't get away."

Already, Leo was pulling out his cell to call the police. He was certain she would head to her home to get her parrots before she tried to get out of town.

The rest of us stared at one another, partly in awe that the plan worked and partly in shock at hearing the confession.

Then Jared sneezed, sneezed again, and began to weep.

EIGHTEEN

Watson hopped in as I opened the driver's side door of the Mini Cooper, bounded over the center console, and then stared out the passenger side window, clearly giving me the cold shoulder—half an hour later and he was still smarting over not being allowed to chase down Petra. That, or he was annoyed about spending such a long time with seven Persian cats. I couldn't quite tell.

I knew one thing. Up until the ten minutes or so I'd spent crammed in the spare hospital room with the cat army, I'd thought my life was ruled by corgi hair. How wrong I had been. Watson might leave a trail of himself behind wherever he went, and I might often be covered head to foot no matter how many sheets of lint rolls I went through, but it was nothing compared to a Persian cat; at least, not compared to seven of them.

"Fred!"

I'd been about to get in the car but paused to look back. Jared was hurrying over from the entrance to the hospital. He'd disappeared mere moments after Petra. I thought he'd gone home. Perhaps he'd just needed time alone in the restroom or something. I smiled at him as he neared, not sure what to say.

He was still red and puffy, but it was impossible to tell how much was from emotion and how much was from allergies. "I'm glad I caught you. I wanted to...." His voice broke. Emotions, it seemed. He spread his arms like he was going to hug me, then paused.

I finished it for him, wrapping my arms around him.

Jared hesitated for a second, then hugged so tight it nearly hurt, and he began to cry once more. It seemed different from when he'd broken down at the end of our confrontation with Petra.

After a few moments, I felt Watson slip out of the car from behind and press himself against our legs.

When Jared finally calmed, he pulled away, wiped his eyes, and withdrew a handkerchief from his pocket to blow his nose. "Thank you." He gave a wobbly smile and wiped his eyes again. "It doesn't bring her back, but it helps. Petra didn't even enter my mind." He issued a sound that resembled a laugh. "I suppose that's ridiculous, considering all the conflict we had over the cats, but I thought it was resolved. She was so happy with those two parrots, and we paid a small fortune for them. Plus, the way it happened with Paulie, I just couldn't.... There wasn't one option that made sense. Not that this made sense. That she'd kill my wife because of cats."

"I don't think she meant to." I shook my head. "I mean, I don't think she planned it. I really do believe it was spur of the moment, not that it helps you, but you couldn't have seen it coming. You can't blame yourself. I think she got that announcement of Belvedere and Cameo, ran into Melody, and it was more than she could handle. Especially after walking in on Paulie like she had. There was no way to predict something like that."

He gave another weird laugh-sob combo. "I wasn't so sure that those next two cats weren't going to do me in either." Jared sucked in a gasp, eyes went wide, and he grabbed my hand in a panic. "I didn't mean it like that. Not at all. I loved Melody. Adored her. I still do."

"I know. That was easy to see." I was tempted to

pull him into another hug but was afraid he'd break again. Though, maybe that would be helpful.

"You probably think I'm awful, putting the cats up for adoption. Petra was right about that." He released my arm to wipe his eyes again. "I know I did it too quickly. I was such a wreck, and the cats were just everywhere, and she... wasn't."

"Jared." I took his hand that time. I wasn't sure what it was about grief and pain that made people feel like they needed to touch each other, but I went with it. "You can't beat yourself up. And it's not a reasonable expectation for you to continue to live with seven cats when clearly your body doesn't want you to."

He nodded, as if he was trying to will himself to believe my words. "I had a cleaning crew come in to deep clean the house, and after they left, I quit taking the pills. And the cats will all go to good homes." That time he laughed for real, and his brown eyes were a little brighter. "Want to hear something ridiculous?"

I nodded.

"After being with them in that hospital room, I decided to take back Angel and Leroy. They were Melody's first cats. We adopted them a few months after we got married. My allergies weren't too bad.

Didn't even need shots, just a bunch of allergy pills. It wasn't until a few years later, when she got more obsessed with them, that my body really revolted."

I wasn't certain what I was supposed to say to that, and I probably chose too blunt of a response. "Are you sure you want to keep them, even only two of them? No one's going to think worse of you."

"I'm sure." His smile was brighter then. "I'm even going to get the cat castle from Paulie. Melody would want that. And, honestly, Angel and Leroy will like it better. I don't think they ever really embraced not being the king and queen of our house. I always thought they resented the other ones. And... it will help keep Melody closer to me for a while."

"I bet you're right. And I know Watson's like that too. I've had a couple of corgi visitors this week, and he's clearly ready to have his house back."

Jared bent and rubbed Watson's sides, and then pressed a kiss to the top of his head. "Thanks to you too, little guy. I'll never forget you chasing that horrible woman."

To my surprise, Watson sat perfectly still, didn't make any move to avoid the affection, even without a promise of a treat.

When Jared stood back up, we looked at each other for a few seconds, an awkwardness falling between us. We hadn't ever spoken before, and suddenly there was nothing left to say.

For a final time, I reached out and squeezed his hand. "Please let us know if you need anything. I guarantee the entire town is here for you."

"Thanks. I'm not sure whether I'm going to stay here or not. Estes was another of Melody's dreams. Though I'd started to fall in love with it. I'm not going to make that decision quickly." He offered another smile, and though sad, it had a bit of ease to it. "Thank you again, Fred. I'll never be able to thank you enough."

Before I could tell him that wasn't needed, he turned and walked away. Watson and I watched him go, and then I gave Watson a matching kiss, ushered him into the car, and we headed home.

Maybe it was a touch morbid, but I curled up later that night in my overstuffed armchair with a copy of *No Cats Allowed*. I always enjoyed Miranda James's cozy mystery series about a cat in the library, but it never seemed more appropriate than in that moment. It was nice to get lost inside a mystery that didn't require me to solve it and didn't put people I loved in danger.

With Watson asleep on one side of the fireplace and Flotsam and Jetsam snoring away on the other, I couldn't ask for a more peaceful end to what had been a short, but emotionally exhausting, few days.

I'd just started to doze off myself when a knock sounded on the door, causing Flotsam and Jetsam to transition from dreamland to utter chaotic hysteria without even a split-second of transition.

Watson and I exchanged a withering look.

"You're fine, boys. I don't think anyone's here to kill us." I patted Flotsam and Jetsam's heads when I met them at the door. It neither soothed nor helped them calm down, not that I expected it would. They were who they were.

I checked the peephole and considered pretending I wasn't home. Of course, considering I'd opened all the windows so I could light a fire, chances were low that would be convincing. Plus, there was no reason to put it off any longer.

Taking a calming breath, as much as one can with two overly fluffy corgis bounding at your feet and a third staring in judgment from across the room, I opened the door and managed to slide out without releasing either of Ursula's eels.

"Joining me on the porch instead of inviting me in, huh? That's not a good sign." Branson took a step back, giving me room, and attempted a wavering smile. His gaze flicked over my flannel nightgown. "Sorry I'm so late. We just finished wrapping things up with Petra."

Maybe he was here to simply give me an update. Though the thought brought with it a wave of relief, I shoved it aside. Even if that was his intention, it was better to get it over with. "She confessed?"

"What choice did she have? She'd just admitted the whole thing in front of a hospital room full of witnesses." He gestured toward the driftwood bench on the other side of my porch. "Care to sit?"

I hesitated long enough that his hand faltered. I didn't want to drag this out.

"Fred...." He sighed.

I walked to the bench and sat down. I didn't want to drag it out, but I also cared about him. Deeply. The anger I'd been feeling so intently at him for the past few days faded to a sense of loss. A stronger one than I would've anticipated. I patted the spot beside me.

Maybe it had been a mistake as hope sprung in his eyes, even visible in the dim glow of the stars and the amber porch light. "Well... you were right again." Branson smiled. "Not that I'm surprised. Charles Franklin didn't hurt Melody after all."

That name had been tumbling around in my head all afternoon, even in the midst of confronting Petra. "I still can't believe he was here, that he's involved. That he was so close and yet...." The suspicion entered, and I narrowed my eyes at Branson, hoping that I would be able to discern the truth. "Is he really dead?"

"Yes." Branson reached out a hand and slipped it over mine. "He really is. Sorry. He won't be able to give you any answers."

Of course not. I'd never been satisfied with the answers we'd received about my father's death. But this had been the first dangling thread to follow that I'd found in all these years, and it was snipped off before I even realized it was there.

Suddenly I was hyperaware of Branson's hand on mine.

I studied it—large, strong, beautiful in a masculine way. Like the man himself. Though part of me was tempted to pull my hand back, I gave in to the comfort of his touch. Allowing myself one brief moment of fantasy that it was going to go differently.

It almost had. Almost....

"I *am* sorry, Fred." Branson's soft, low voice brought my attention back to his face. "Now I hope you understand why I had to cut you out of this one.

I couldn't take the risk, not with Paulie in witness protection. It wasn't even something we shared with the rest of the police force."

I nodded slowly, considering. And while I'd already crossed that bridge in my mind, I let it play out one more time. "That part does make sense to me, Branson. It really does."

"It's not that I didn't trust you. I did. I *do*." He hurried on, sounding a little more frantic than I'd heard him before. "I didn't have a choice in the matter."

"I said that it makes sense to me. I wasn't lying." I spared one more glance at our hands, then pulled mine away before meeting his gaze again. "However"—I tried to keep my voice friendly and calm, but also strong—"you did have a choice in how you handled it."

He shook his head. "No, I really didn't. It's protocol. I—"

"*Yes*, you did." I took a brief breath, feeling my temper spike. I was not going to let this descend into an argument. "You did have a choice. You could have said exactly what you told me right now. That due to protocol, due to another person's safety, you literally could not share any detail of the case. You even could've told me that my involvement would put another person at risk. Though... I think I've proven that wasn't true."

He started to speak, but I shook my head.

"Instead of that, you demanded. In ways that were rather unkind and belittling. You told me to keep my nose out of it, told me to sell books, told me you would pursue legal action."

"Fred, that's my job. I was doing my job." He didn't sound frustrated, simply matter-of-fact.

"Okay." I'd already made up my mind, but a new wave of peace swept over me. It was just confirmation. "I'm not going to argue about that. And in the truest sense of the word, yes, you were doing your job. But again, it was the way you did your job that I'm not okay with."

He started to reach for my hand again but stopped midmotion. "I'm sorry about your feelings. I really am. But—"

"This isn't about hurting my feelings." I sat a little straighter, and though my anger spiked, it only deepened my resolve and sense of calm. "It's about respect. It's about promises I've made that I will never allow myself to be treated in belittling ways again. At least not by people who have a certain elevated position in my life."

Branson cocked his head, as if in disbelief. "Are you saying that you're ending things with us? We're barely getting started. After all these months, we're merely getting started. And you're ending it... because of this?"

I couldn't believe how shocked he sounded. "Yes. That's exactly what I'm saying."

Temper flared behind his eyes, but it was gone quickly. Even in that flash, there was no sense of danger or threat. I knew, even then, that Branson's promise was true. I would always be safe with him. All well and good, but if I was ever going to love again, I wanted a lot more than safety.

"Fred, I'm sorry. I will ask for your forgiveness, and I will promise to do better in the future." He did take my hand again then. Forceful, but not aggressively. "I love you."

I balked. Of all the things I'd anticipated him saying when we eventually had this conversation, I hadn't predicted that.

"I do. I love you, Winifred Page." He leaned a little closer, his eyes earnest. "Let me make it right. Let me prove it to you."

For one electric heartbeat, a sliver of doubt entered.

He loved me. I could see it clearly. It wasn't even

a moment of panic or fear of loss that made him think he did. Branson loved me.

And... I loved him. But with him sitting there, ready to make that leap, I realized why we were barely getting started even after all those months. And it wasn't simply because I'd not been looking for a relationship, nor because I hadn't wanted one, though I hadn't.

I loved Branson Wexler, but not in the way that he loved me. Not in the way I should.

As if that wasn't clear enough, the realization that followed pounded every nail in place. Even if I did love him in that way, after the past few days, it wouldn't have mattered. I didn't expect perfection in a relationship. I didn't expect there not to be conflict or arguments or fights. But I'd already had a marriage where my other half didn't truly see me as equal to himself. And even though Branson might not be aware of it, he'd revealed, at least in some part of his heart, that was true for him as well.

I folded my hand on top of his so it was enclosed and looked at him—really looked into his eyes. "I love you too, but not in the way that will make this work." I started to list the reasons, then decided it didn't matter. "We're not a match, you and me. I thought we might have been. I wasn't sure, but I thought that maybe…. But I was wrong."

He winced again. Confusion crossed his features, then pain. "I really am sorry. We can start again. We can…."

His words trailed off as I shook my head. "It's done, Branson. I'm not angry, and we can still…." I started to say still be friends, but I hated that. Everyone hated hearing that. Though it was true, I hoped Branson and I could be friends. But this wasn't the time to go there. "I don't want to hurt you, but… it's over."

There was a bark from inside the cabin. Watson. One sharp, clear bark.

He always knew. Just that touching base of companionship. Letting me know that he was there. And chances were high, telling me I had better wrap it up quickly so I could get him a snack.

A moment later the other two went into hysterics, barking, yapping, and pawing at the back of the front door.

The noise seemed to break the spell, and Branson shook his head, pulled his hand free, and then stood. When he looked down at me, both his expression and his voice were kind. "I hope you change your mind. I'll be here if you do."

I started to say that I wouldn't. That he shouldn't wait. Though true enough, it seemed cruel, so I simply nodded.

After another pause of hesitation, he turned, walked off the porch, and got into his police cruiser.

I watched him drive away, disappear into the forest that lay between my cabin and the housing developments that led into town. Though there was a lingering sense of loss, the peace remained. It was right.

Peace was the furthest thing from the mind of Flotsam and Jetsam as I walked back into the cabin. Clearly, they thought I was being murdered, or feared they were missing all the fun.

Watson sat beside the overstuffed armchair, waiting for me.

"What do you want us to call you, Simon or Paulie?" Katie placed a platter of assorted baked goods in the center of the table and sat down between Leo and Athena.

"I've been thinking about that a lot, actually." Paulie chose a ham-and-cheese croissant from the options, then transferred it to his plate. "When I first went into the program, being called Paulie nearly drove me insane. But now...." His gaze traveled around the table to each of us in turn before a blush rose to his cheeks and he refocused on the food. "Well... I kinda like the life Paulie has made for himself here. I decided that I'm going to change my middle name legally to Paulie, so I'll be Simon Paulie Bezor. But my friends will call me Paulie."

"That sounds perfect." Leo smacked him on the

back. "That means you're staying? You're not going back to Illinois?"

"Oh, he's staying." Leah sounded partly irritated and partly amused. "Mom and Dad and John have all tried to talk him into moving back home, but he insists that he is home. At least we can have Christmases and holidays together again." Seeing Leah and Paulie side by side made me wonder how anyone who'd observed them together hadn't instantly realized they were siblings. "Although, *I'm* thinking about moving here."

"No." Paulie's head shot up, and his tone was sharp. He flushed again and softened his tone. "We've talked about this. When Mom, Dad, and John go home next week, you're going with them. You can come and visit every so often, but you can't move here."

The entire table stared at him. It wasn't like Paulie to be so dogmatic.

Athena patted his hand. Before this, they'd seemed like friends, but since he'd been hurt, she'd taken on more and more of a mothering role, even with his actual mother in town. "Paulie, Leah is a grown woman. She can move here if she wants."

Though he still sounded rather embarrassed, Paulie shook his head. "No. Her life is there. She doesn't need to disrupt it for me." It looked like Leah wasn't going to argue, but Paulie made a sweeping gesture over the bakery. "I can't believe you all did this for me. And I can't believe everyone showed up."

"The entire town showed up!" Leo jumped in, clearly trying to help Paulie change the subject. "You're the current hot topic and star of the town."

"They probably think it's weird that you all did a Little Mermaid theme, but I *love* it." He grinned at Katie and me. "The eels that you guys made to hold up the Welcome Home banner over the door are pretty phenomenal."

I was pleased he liked them, though I would've been shocked if he hadn't. "We can't take credit for those. Beulah, from the scrapbook store, made them."

Paulie had gotten out of the hospital early that morning, and Katie and I had opened the Cozy Corgi and bakery for a welcome home celebration. I kept thinking that our shops couldn't get any busier, but they could. The entire town, and every tourist within earshot, had shown up.

"Of course everyone showed up!" Leah threw her arm around Paulie and squeezed, thankfully letting the argument go. "They love you. That says a lot about these people. They're smart and see what a wonderful man you are."

Paulie blushed, though he was clearly pleased. "Well... it's very sweet."

"Excuse me." Someone tapped my shoulder, and I swiveled around in my chair. A woman I didn't recognize pointed to where Watson and Pearl were curled up together over in the corner. "Someone told me you own the place, and I'm not sure if you noticed, but there are two *dogs* over there. And in your bookshop, there are two other dogs, wild ones, running amok. There's also a very hairy orange cat."

"Thank you for letting me know." I had to bite the inside of my cheek for a second to keep from chuckling, and nodded over to the corner. "The corgi there is Watson. He's the mascot of the bookshop and bakery, and all the others are his... friends." I wasn't sure if Watson would agree with that statement. Definitely about Pearl, but I wasn't certain, even after all their time together, if Flotsam and Jetsam had moved into friendship territory or had merely made it off Watson's hit list. Cinnamon was little more than an irritant to him.

"Oh...." The tourist looked from Watson and Pearl to the pastries we were devouring to the bakery counter. She blinked. "All right, then." She wandered off.

Katie giggled. "How much do you want to bet

the health department gets a call in about three minutes?"

"Maybe we should save her some time and introduce her to the health inspector, who's chowing down on éclairs." I pointed to the scarecrow-thin man at the table nearest to Watson and Pearl.

Paulie caught my arm and pulled me aside before he, Flotsam, and Jetsam headed out to rejoin Leah and the rest of their family for dinner. "I can't thank you enough, Fred. I also can't tell you how much your friendship means."

"You don't need to thank me for anything. Besides, *I* didn't find out who hurt you, only who killed Melody."

"Thank you for looking into that too, but that isn't what I meant." We were at the base of the steps, and he smiled over into the mystery room where Watson was perched on top of the antique sofa, tauntingly removed from where the chunkier Flotsam and Jetsam were able to reach. "I actually meant for taking care of my boys. I know they aren't easy. But it means so much. And thanks for throwing the welcome-back party too, of course."

"I'm sure they'll be excited to be back home." I

gave him an awkward hug. "But you don't need to thank us. We love you. And we're so glad you're okay."

He nodded, emotion clear on his face as he pulled back from the hug. For a second, I thought he was going to walk away, but he paused and cleared his throat. "Will you forgive me for not telling you who I really was?"

"Paulie!" I gripped his hand. "There's nothing to forgive. It wasn't like you sought to deceive us. You were simply trying to stay alive. No one thinks nega-tively of you for that. And we're glad you're staying."

He studied me as if judging my sincerity. "Okay. Thank you. I'm glad." Again it looked like he was going to leave, and again he held back. "Fred?"

His tone had changed, and a chill went through me. "Yeah?"

He held my gaze in an unusually direct stare. "There are still things I can't tell you. There are still things in Estes that you don't know about."

I started to laugh, thinking, maybe hoping, he was being silly, but my laughter died instantly. "What do you mean?"

Paulie considered and then shook his head. "I can't tell you. But I didn't want to keep lying to you. I know I'm not completely being honest, but maybe it helps if I let you know that there are secrets that I can't say. Maybe that's not exactly lying."

I started to tell him he could trust me with anything, then realized he was doing exactly what I'd told Branson he should've done. But still, I had to ask. "Are you in danger?"

Again, he had to consider, which worried me. Finally, he shook his head. "No... no." He met my gaze once more. "And neither are you. If I thought you were, I'd tell you, no matter the consequences. And I promise, if I ever think that you are in danger, I will. I'll tell you."

Once more that chill rushed through me. It took all my willpower not to demand an explanation. "Okay... I'm not really sure what to say to that. I guess... thank you for telling me."

He nodded somberly and then forced a smile. "Say, did you ever take a picture with Watson wearing the hat with the stack of books that you ordered?" He shook his head. "Wait a minute, it came in, but you never picked it up, did you?"

It was hard to pull myself back to the moment, hard to think of dog costumes with what he'd just said. "Um... no... I never did pick it up. That was why I was coming over that day, when I found you and Melody."

"Let me go get it real quick. I'll be right back." Paulie started to rush off. "Come on, boys."

Flotsam and Jetsam tore away from Watson, who collapsed in relief on top of the sofa.

"No, you don't need to do that," I called out to Paulie before he got too far.

He looked back at me questioningly.

"If you don't mind, just sell it to someone else. Watson has been a true champ through this whole thing." I smiled over at him. "No more outfits for him, even if the picture would be completely adorable."

That night, for the first time in what felt like forever, though it hadn't actually been all that long, the cabin was truly and completely peaceful.

Watson and I had dinner, and then we curled up in our normal spots by the fire. He drifted off, and I started to read. I didn't even make it a chapter before I put the book down and slid out of the chair and sat cross-legged on the floor beside him.

He stared up at me with a grunt, irritated at his nap being disrupted.

"Sorry, buddy." I ruffled his fur. "I just needed to be close to you."

He narrowed those warm chocolate eyes of his, and I could see he was considering trotting away to sleep in peace. Instead, with an indulgent huff, he lowered his head to my lap.

"Thanks, my little grump." I stroked his sides. "You really are something special. Thanks for putting up with Flotsam and Jetsam invading your home this week. It's nice to have our serenity back, isn't it? To only be you and me again."

He sighed, which I chose to interpret as agreement. Though it just as easily could have been him thinking, *Good grief, will this woman ever shut up?*

I sat there for a long time, with the fire blazing and the cool mountain breeze coming through the open windows. Sat there until my hips and legs went numb from the hardwood floor. I didn't care. It was a perfect moment. And I had all I needed.

Friends and family. My dream business located in a town I adored.

That was all vital and wonderful.

But really... moments like this—quiet, calm, and peaceful. Moments like this—with Watson, who most would say was *just* a dog. I knew he was so, so much more. All you had to do was ask him. *These* were the moments I treasured the most.

## ALASTAIR TYLER

As I've mentioned before, Watson was inspired by a very special corgi in my life. A corgi named Alastair. I gave Watson Alastair's exact personality save for two qualities. Watson is a touch more brave, and likes a vast many more people than Alastair would ever dream of being appropriate.

In the midst of writing *Chaotic Corgis*, my sweet little man, Alastair, passed away. Finishing this novel has been bittersweet. Writing about Watson during this loss has been a strange sort of comfort. While I disappear into the world of Fred and Estes Park, Alastair is still with me, and it is lovely.

I don't share this to be melancholy or make you sad at the end of what I hope was a fun and enjoyable book for you. I simply want you to know that Watson comes from a very real place and has a lot to live up to. And I'm so, so very glad that in some way, those of you who read and enjoy the Cozy Corgi series will get to carry Alastair with you as I do. Though if he met you in real life, he more than likely would've sniffed your hand, if that, and then sauntered away—unless you offered a treat—it warms my heart that you all get to love him like I do.

This book, and every one hereafter will be dedicated to Alastair, and his spirit will continue to give Watson all of his charm and grumpy personality, and in this way, he'll continue to have adventure after adventure.

Katie's (Lois's) Dog Treat recipe provided by:

4128 Hooker Street, Denver, CO 80211
(303) 877-2704

---

Biscotti Hound makes several other flavors of dog biscuits (including peanut butter).  We also make Gelato, Happy Birthday Bones, & Pupcakes.  Biscotti Hound specializes in semi-custom dog birthday cakes.  Please call us 24 hours in advance to place your order!

Click the links for more Biscotti Hound perfection:

BiscottiHound.com

Biscotti Hound Facebook Page

(Corgi cookie jar by Montana Silversmiths
and tie by stahl.etsy.com)

## Ingredients:

8 cups whole wheat flour (adjust as needed)

*NOT BLEACHED FLOUR*

1 ½ cups old-fashioned oats

2 tablespoons cinnamon

3 cups peanut butter

4 cups **hot** water (adjust as needed)

## Directions:

**Pre-heat oven to 275 degrees.**

**Preheat oven to 275 degrees.**

Combine all ingredients in a standing mixer (with the dough hook) in the following order: **Hot**

**water, peanut butter, cinnamon, oats, flour. Dough should be moist.**

Roll out dough to 1/4 inch thickness. Stamp out with your favorite cookie cutter shape. Place biscuits on parchment-lined baking sheets for more evenly baked biscuits. Bake all trays at the same time.

Bake at 275 for 1 hour and 15 minutes or until done. When done, turn off oven and leave trays of biscuits in oven to cool down. The biscuits will be hard and crunchy!

Store biscuits in a cool dry place. Do not place in a plastic container with a tight lid, as they can mold. A tin container or ziplock (not completely zipped tight) works best! Biscuits can also be frozen.

## ABOUT THE AUTHOR

Reading the Cozy Corgi series is pretty much all you need to know about Mildred. In real life, she's obsessed with everything she writes about: Corgis, Books, Cozy Mountain Towns, and Baked Goods. She's not obsessed with murder, however. At least not at her own hands (nor paid for... no contract killing here). But since childhood, starting with Nancy Drew, trying to figure out who-dun-it has played a formative role in her personality. Having Fred and Watson stroll into her mind was a touch of kismet.

Website: Mildredabbott.com

Dear Reader:

Thank you so much for reading *Chaotic Corgis*. If you enjoyed Fred and Watson's adventure, I would greatly appreciate a review on Amazon and Goodreads. Please drop me a note on Facebook or on my website (MildredAbbott.com) whenever you like. I'd love to hear from you.

I also wanted to mention the elephant in the room... or the over-sugared corgi, as it were. Watson's personality is based around one of my own corgis, Alastair. He's the sweetest little guy in the world, and, like Watson, is a bit of a grump. Also, like Watson (and every other corgi to grace the world with their presence), he lives for food. In the Cozy

Corgi series, I'm giving Alastair the life of his dreams through Watson. Just like I don't spend my weekends solving murders, neither does he spend his days snacking on scones and unending dog treats. But in the books? Well, we both get to live out our fantasies. If you are a corgi parent, you already know your little angel shouldn't truly have free rein of the pastry case, but you can read them snippets of Watson's life for a pleasant bedtime fantasy.

And don't miss book seven, *Quarrelsome Quartz*, coming July 2018.

Much love, Mildred

PS: I'd also love it if you signed up for my newsletter. That way you'll never miss a new release. You won't hear from me more than once a month, nobody needs that many newsletters!

Newsletter link: Mildred Abbott Newsletter Signup

ACKNOWLEDGMENTS

A special thanks to Agatha Frost, who gave her blessing and her wisdom. If you haven't already, you simply MUST read Agatha's Peridale Cafe Cozy Mystery series. They are absolute perfection.

The biggest and most heartfelt gratitude to Katie Pizzolato, for her belief in my writing career and being the inspiration for the character of the same name in this series. Thanks to you, Katie, our beloved baker, has completely stolen both mine and Fred's heart!

Desi, I couldn't imagine an adventure without you by my side. A.J. Corza, you have given me the corgi covers of my dreams. A huge, huge thank you to all of the lovely souls who proofread the ARC versions and helped me look somewhat literate (in completely random order): Melissa Brus, Cinnamon, Ron Perry, Rob Andresen-Tenace, Anita Ford, Nicole Davis, TL Travis, Victoria Smiser, Lucy Campbell, Sue Paulsen, and Lisa Jackson. Thank you all, so very, very much!

A further and special thanks to some of my dear readers and friends who support my passion: Andrea Johnson, Fiona Wilson, Katie Pizzolato, Maggie Johnson, Marcia Gleason, Rob Andresen- Tenace, Robert Winter, Jason R., Victoria Smiser, Kristi Browning, and those of you who wanted to remain anonymous. You make a huge, huge difference in my life and in my ability to continue to write. I'm humbled and grateful beyond belief! So much love to you all!

# QUARRELSOME QUARTZ

## COMING JULY 2018

Made in the USA
Las Vegas, NV
04 September 2023

77052488R00184